The Limit

The Limit
Ada Leverson

MINT EDITIONS

The Limit was first published in 1911.

This edition published by Mint Editions 2021.

ISBN 9781513132365

Published by Mint Editions®

 MINT
EDITIONS

minteditionbooks.com

Publishing Director: Jennifer Newens
Design & Production: Rachel Lopez Metzger
Project Manager: Micaela Clark
Typesetting: Westchester Publishing Services

Contents

I

Valentia

R omer, are you listening?"

"Valentia, do I ever do anything else?"

"I've almost decided and absolutely made up my mind that it will look ever so much better if you don't go with me to Harry's dinner after all."

"Really?"

"Yes. We two—you *and* I—always seem to make such an enormous family party! Of course, I know we have to go about in these huge batches sometimes—to your mother, and that sort of thing, but in this case it will look better not."

Valentia made this rather ungracious suggestion, looking so pretty, so serious, and yet with such a conciliating smile that it would have been almost impossible for even the most touchy person to have been offended.

The tall, significant-looking husband stopped in his stroll across the room.

It was a charming room, with pale grey walls and a pale green carpet, and very little in it except, let in as a panel, a delicate low-toned portrait of the mistress of the house, vaguely appearing through vaporous curtains, holding pale flowers, and painted with a rather mysterious effect by that talented young amateur, her cousin, Harry de Freyne. It had been his sole success in art, and had been exhibited at the Grafton Galleries under the name of The Gilded Lily. No one had ever known or was ever likely to know whether the title referred to the decorative, if botanically impossible, blossom in her hand, or to the golden hair of the seductive sitter.

Romer Wyburn paused a moment—he always paused before speaking—and then said very slowly—

"Oh! Really? You think it will look better if I don't go with you?"

He invariably spoke with the greatest deliberation, and with no expression whatever.

"Oh yes, dear, I'm sure it would," she repeated coaxingly.

"Do you mean if you go without me?"

"What else can I mean?"

"It'll look better, you think; eh? Is that the idea?"

He sat down opposite the portrait, lighted a cigarette, and thought. Then he said with ruminating interest—

"I don't see why. Why will it look so much better for me not to go with you?"

"Oh, Romer dear, really! It's one of those things that are almost impossible to explain. Oh, if you'd only do just what I advise—if you'd only *go* by me, and not want these long tedious explanations, how much better it would be! You see, Harry is giving this dinner *on purpose* so that Daphne shall meet Van Buren by accident. You know all about Van Buren, *the* Van Buren—the millionaire, who turns out to be a dear creature and quite charming! and has taken the *greatest* fancy to Harry, and clings on to him, and keeps on and on asking him to ask him to meet people. You must own it would be rather jolly for Daphne, because, of course, you can't *think* how he's run after—I mean Van Buren—and he isn't an ordinary American snob, and it really and truly isn't only his millionairishness, but he's a real person, and good-looking and nice as well; and though, Heaven knows, I'm as romantic as anybody—for myself—I wouldn't be so selfish as to be romantic for her too, and I can't help feeling it's our duty, being in the place of parents to her, to give the angel a sporting chance! Of course, the point is, Van Buren has told Harry he only likes nice English girls very well brought up, and he wants to settle down in England, and he thinks that any relation of Harry's must be perfect; and, naturally, I'm pleased. I feel exactly like a mother to Daphne, although she's only six years younger."

"Well, that's all right. I see all that."

Romer seemed rather bored, as men naturally are at a long catalogue of another man's advantages. "Now, look here. Why would it look better for me not to go?"

There was some excuse for his insistence on this point, for in a superficial way Romer was very effective, fair and good-looking, well-made and distinguished; but the entire absence of all expression from his empty, regular face, and of all animation from his dry, colourless voice and manner, soon counteracted the effectiveness. Valentia often said that Romer should never do more than walk through a room or look in for a few minutes where there were other people—even at a club—and then go away immediately, when he would leave a striking impression. If he stayed longer he became alarming. His personality was so extraordinarily *nil* that it was quite oppressive. Obviously kind and not in the least pompous, yet his silence made him formidable, especially to most of his wife's friends who, though they could hardly be reproached with want of pluck as a general rule, had one great fear in life—the fear of being bored. It was on this ground that they were all terrified of Romer.

"Don't you think, Romer, if we both go it will look too marked? Almost as if we were vulgarly trying to get Daphne married? A horrid idea! Besides, if you don't turn up Harry can ask some one amusing in your place. You see, he's promised to show Van Buren *interesting* people. . . No, darling, I don't mean it in that way. I'm sure you're interesting enough, but I mean queer people, and celebrities and things. That's what Van Buren wants, and that's what he must have. And that's one reason why he's so delighted with Harry, because Harry can get them all, through being a sort of artist, you see. What a good thing, after all, that he didn't drift into diplomacy! As he's an American you can't expect Van Buren to be really modern, and he has all the old-fashioned ideas about what *he* calls culture. He wants to go in for being intellectual and artistic and knowing what he calls people with brains who really count. I mean he wants to meet people like Seymour Hicks and Waller, and Thomas Hardy, and so on, and not only celebrities and people who have made their name, but even people with a future, and, in fact, any peculiar, well-educated creatures—anything out of the way."

Romer looked rather dazed.

"Really? Then will Hicks or Hardy be asked in my place?"

Valentia laughed. "Don't be so absurdly literal and hopelessly idiotic, darling! No, of course not. But I dare say Harry will get—well—perhaps Rathbone, the tattooed man, his Oxford friend."

"Really! And will this chap's being tattooed make the party go off better?"

"Oh yes, Romer dear; in a sort of way, because it makes him interesting, although you can't see it. When he was quite young he was always having lifelong passions for people, and being tattooed in their honour. He has blue chain bracelets with initials on his left wrist, and a heart and an anchor with other initials on his right arm, and a flight of swallows—oh, and goodness knows what! In fact, when you come to think of it Mr. Rathbone is really a kind of serial story—with illustrations. I wonder Lord Northcliffe doesn't bring him out in monthly parts!" She laughed again. "Harry might even get Hereford

Vaughan, the man who has written all the plays that are going on now. Harry knows him quite well, and Van Buren would be so pleased."

"Does Daphne want to many this American chap?"

"Good gracious, no! The idea! Why, she doesn't even know him! . . . Yes, of course she does, naturally."

"Oh!"

Romer, though he never by any chance smiled at his wife's careless irresponsible chatter, nor laughed at her trivial jests, took the deepest interest in them, and would listen, as if under a charm, by the hour, to subtleties and frivolities that one would never have imagined he would enjoy. Sometimes the faint shadow of a smile would illuminate his face like a cold ray of wintry moonlight, but that was when she had ceased speaking. The smile was the effect of having watched the sparkle of her grey eyes, the expression of her pretty mouth, and her brilliant, sunshiny grace.

"It's very sweet of Harry," she said thoughtfully, "to do all this for me. It's all for me, or rather it's all for Daphne; he's so fond of Daphne."

"Really? Why doesn't he marry her himself?"

She looked surprised and blushed slightly.

"Harry? Why, he never marries!"

"He doesn't as a rule, I know," Romer admitted.

"Then, why should he make an exception for Daphne? He's fond of her—of us—in fact, devoted—just like a brother. Not that I ever saw a devoted brother. Besides, Harry's made to be a bachelor, and he isn't well off enough to marry."

"Really? Hard up? Poor chap! Never saw any sign of it."

"Hard up? No; how like you! Of course, he has plenty of money, for *him*, but he spends it all, poor boy. Anyhow, of course, he's not really rich like Van Buren. It's on a totally different scale—a different sort of thing altogether. But, of course, Van Buren may not care for Daphne; people have such funny tastes; and not only that, but if he adores and worships the ground she treads on I shan't let her dream of marrying him unless she absolutely returns it—at least, unless she likes him fairly well."

All this seemed to absorb Romer, and after a pause he said—

"I suppose you'll get Daphne a new dress for Harry's beano?"

Valentia smiled pityingly.

"Yes, of course, you would think that. No! Why, that would be *l'enfance de l'art*! First of all, Daphne looks ever so much better when she's dressed really simply, not the latest fashion; on the very verge of dowdiness! It suits her—shows her off. It would be silly to dress her up like a doll or make her look *endimanchée* on Thursday, or arranged and got up expensively, on purpose for Van Buren. I wouldn't, for instance, for anything, let her wear her new tulle dress from Armand! He'd see through it. Besides, I want her to contrast with me as if I'd taken any amount of trouble about my own appearance and none about hers. It'll make him pity her a little, and think how well she'd look in the sort of clothes he could give her. Besides, I myself am not going to be very smart—just tidy."

"Paquin?"

"How clever of you to guess! Well, now I must go and see Harry and hear all about the dinner, and tell him how sorry you are you can't come. And you're going to lunch at the Club, aren't you? And won't you go and dine with your mother on that evening?"

"I may as well."

"*Do*, Romer dear! I can't bear you to neglect her, although I never think it's safe to let you dine with her without me. She always takes advantage of my absence to be horrid about me, and then you *will* defend me, although I've implored you not to heaps of times, and then you quarrel. If, this time, she says I'm frivolous and worldly and an utter fool and very deep, you must agree with every word. I'm so fond of her, she's such a dear thing, it's too bad to worry her by contradicting her, and she has such a vile temper! Telephone and invite yourself—a pressing invitation, and give her my very best love."

Romer promised all she asked and then went out to the Club.

Valentia watched him through the window as he went. She thought he looked very well through a window, and ought by rights always to be seen in that way—as it were, under glass. She felt quite proud of him, of his smart appearance. In his way, he was an elaborate dandy, and spent years at his tailor's, slowly choosing the right thing. She remembered she had married him chiefly because of his fine presence and mysterious silence. She had thought at the time there must be so much at the back of it all, so much in him. He was in love with her and seemed difficult to understand. What could be more attractive? And now—well, he was ideally kind and good-natured. And she certainly felt sometimes that she couldn't even yet quite make him out. Then she gave a slight sigh, went to the door and called Daphne.

Daphne came in, trimming a hat. She had lived with the Wyburns ever since their marriage five years ago, and Valentia, having no children and a most passionately tender disposition—far too much natural affection to expend on Romer alone—lavished devotion on her sister. And Daphne was so nice and so pretty, almost as pretty as herself, in a satisfactorily different way. Valentia with her short straight features, grey eyes under dark brows, low forehead almost hidden by wavy fair hair, and a mouth curved and curled into subtle and complicated lines, was the type loved by Rossetti and Burne-Jones. She had a wonderful fair complexion, against which her long eyelashes showed, when she looked down, dark and effective, and though she was rather tall, slim and very modishly dressed, she never looked like a fashion-plate and had no air of being a mere mannequin for clothes, but seemed essentially real, with a suggestion in her personality of a beauty at once pagan and spiritual—the pagan predominating. Her pictorial appearance had no doubt made easier the artist's task, and the pale exquisite portrait had truly been described as a whispering likeness.

Daphne, who was not quite eighteen, was a good deal taller, and more slender. She had dark brown eyes, smooth dark hair, parted in the middle, a rather bright colour and features of the classic type. Her chin was rather long, and she had a brilliant, sudden smile, and all the attractive freshness and slight abruptness of her age, with an occasionally subdued air, caused by the shadow that had fallen on their youth by the death of their beautiful mother. Her gentle grace and touch of premeditated *naïveté* made her charming. Beyond question she would be a great success.

"Romer can't go on Thursday," Valentia said, taking the needle and hat out of her sister's hand and beginning to sew. "I must go and see Harry and tell him to get some one else. Really, Daphne, you go too far! It's all very well to be clever with your needle, but you needn't tear a Lewis hat to pieces and turn it inside out without asking my advice."

"Oh, I wasn't! I was only squashing in the brim and trying to make the hat smaller. It seems to have got larger since I put it away."

"Don't be perfectly absurd, darling. It's because you've been seeing smaller hats lately."

"Oh yes, I see. Who's going instead of Romer?"

"How should I know? We'll see."

"It's just as you like, darling," said Daphne in her level voice; "but in case the American hates me, and I hate him, and Harry's talking to you all the time, and I'm frightened of the celebrities, isn't anything going to be done for me?"

"Of course not. What do you want? That Foster boy again? Don't look down and blush, it makes me sick. All right, perhaps, if there's room. He's a nice, decorative boy, but remember they don't dance at dinner, and that's the only thing he can do."

"Indeed it isn't!" cried Daphne.

"I'm very sorry to hear it. Suppose Foster's engaged, or at Aldershot?"

"He won't be. It's too sweet of Romer not going. Did you marry him because you knew he would do whatever you told him?"

"I don't think it was that so much," said Valentia, thoughtfully, trying on the hat in front of the glass. "I thought he was a strong silent man, a man with an orange up his sleeve, as it were. But I've never seen the orange."

"How funny of you! I should hate a mysterious person. You don't want your husband to be a kind of conjurer."

"Yes, I do, as long as he doesn't wear a conjurer's evening dress. I like being surprised. Now let's go and surprise Harry at his studio; we must be quick, he's expecting us."

II

HARRY

Harry de Freyne stood in his usual position, smoking a cigarette, and leaning a little forward, with his back to the mirror as if to resist the temptation of looking into it. The family good looks were acutely accentuated in this young man. He had the smooth, glossy dark hair, white teeth, and speaking dark grey eyes that women like; clearly-cut features, and the rather prominent chin, generally and mistakenly supposed to show strength of character. His pleasant, clean-shaven, slightly sunburnt face bore an expression of animation with a certain humorous anxiety natural in a man who was generally a good deal in debt and always a little in love. Further he had the advantage of a tall, strong yet supple figure, with a natural grace of movement and much personal charm. Harry knew he was good-looking and did not undervalue the fact, but regarded it solely as an asset, not as a private satisfaction. He regarded everything as an asset. He was no fop, although he wore a single eye-glass rather as a concession to some ideal of dandyism than as a help to clear vision. He could see remarkably well, with or without it.

The long Empire mirror was placed above a delightful early English large open fireplace, in which burnt a Parisian-looking wood fire. Harry was the possessor of a fine—indeed, a magnificent studio, full of good old things, chiefly other people's, and bad new things, principally his own. The theory that all bad art is the result of sincere feeling was certainly not exemplified in his case. The portrait of his cousin that had been regarded as so full of promise was, as he always, said, the only decent piece of work he had ever done. He had been educated for diplomacy, and learnt eight languages, some of which he spoke fluently, and in all of which he could look with expression.

The room was no mere exhibition of bric-à-brac, but was a cosy, shadowy, miscellaneous place, not without an ecclesiastical touch here and there. One felt every subject could be gone into there, from stockbroking to love, and that everything could be done there, whether it was praying, eating, singing, or flirting—everything except perhaps painting.

When the servant announced Mrs. Wyburn and Miss de Freyne

one might have fancied Harry looked slightly disappointed, but he greeted the pretty creatures with suitable effusion and high spirits.

They both sat down rather carefully in the corner seats by the fire.

"Romer can't come, he's dining with his mother," announced Valentia. "He ought to, you know, now and then."

"I don't like her," said Daphne, "she abuses every one."

"I know she does, but she's really not so bad, dear, all the same; there are many worse. She's rather spiteful, but warmhearted—awfully kind if you break your leg," said Valentia.

"But you don't break your leg," said Harry.

"Oh, sometimes you do. At any rate you might. Don't encourage Daphne to argue, Harry. Who did you say you'd ask instead if we couldn't get Romer?"

"Rathbone's just written to accept in his place," said Harry, taking out a letter. "But—don't you think we could persuade Romer if we tried hard? However, you know best."

He took out a list. "Hereford Vaughan, Van Buren, Rathbone and me—that's four; you two, Lady Walmer, and Miss Luscombe, the actress. I think that'll do."

"Lady Walmer?" repeated Valentia. "Why?"

"And a real actress!" murmured Daphne.

"Not a real actress. She's walked on at all the principal theatres in London, and somebody's always going to take a theatre for her, but there's no danger. I told Van Buren that on the stage they think she's in society, and in society they believe she's on the stage. And he thinks it's real cute, and an extraordinary English type."

"How are you getting on with him?"

"Beautifully,—if he weren't so beastly intelligent and inquisitive. He always wants to know all the news and all the latest gossip. What do you think he asked me last night? Why Big Ben was called Big Ben! How on earth should I know!"

"Big who?"

"Not big anybody;—the place, the thing;—the clock. He said no doubt I must think him dreadfully ignorant for not knowing, but he felt he must ask."

Smiling at the recollection, Harry lighted another cigarette.

"What did you say?" Daphne asked.

"If it had been the afternoon I think I'd have taken the risk and told him I didn't know, but as it was the evening—he always gets rather excited in the evening after dinner and so much Perrier water,—walking back to the Ritz in the moonlight, and talking about London, I invented a long story.—No, he won't repeat it, don't be frightened; it was really rather awful; and when Van Buren gives you his word of honour not to tell a thing. . ."

"You're all right! That must be a great help," said Valentia sympathetically.

"It shows he has a nice loyal nature," Daphne remarked. "I admire that sort of thing very much."

"A nice loyal nature! I should think he has! He hates spreading scandal, and he wouldn't say a single word now to take away the character of Big Ben—if it was—"

"What?"

"Oh, if it was ever so! You ought to make Daphne wear one of those thin tulle veils to match her hat. They're jolly—you can get them at that shop close to me."

"Oh, she needn't, she's going to be manicured, and she's coming back here for me in a quarter of an hour."

"Good-bye, darling," said Daphne, standing up, and she made a kind of face, which Valentia understood to mean the word Foster.

"What is the child playing at?" said Harry. "If you two have a code it would be as well to learn it."

"All right," said Valentia to Daphne.

Harry walked with her to the door and she ran out, saying, "I won't be long."

"She wants Foster, the baby Guardsman," explained Valentia.

"Oh, why didn't you say so at first? Of course I suppose they've arranged it. At any rate it's as good as done. Then there must be one more woman. But never mind now."

Harry sat down beside her and said, in a different voice—he had a very good voice, especially when he spoke caressingly—

"How interesting you are! One of your eyebrows is a little thicker than the other."

"Oh, Harry! . . ."

"How are we all going to get home that evening?"

"What do you think?" she asked.

"Well, it's like this, as you may say. We'll all meet at the Ritz and dine there. Good. Then we drive in separate vehicles to here, and have some music. Then I see you both home, and—well, I think that's all. It's not much."

"I don't quite like the way Lady Walmer looks at you, Harry."

"Oh, Valentia! If it comes to that, how do you fondly imagine I shall like the way Rathbone is sure to look at you?"

"Oh, Harry! Why, he's tattooed!"

"You see," went on Harry seriously, "I really am making a dash for it about Daphne. She'll really be happy with Van Buren, and *I* shall be ever so much happier,—with Van Buren and everyone else,—because, through Daphne being always with you, I never see you alone for one single second."

"Oh, you exaggerate, Harry!"

"I know I do. I don't see you for half a second."

"Romer has been so nice lately," she answered gently.

"Very amusing, I suppose?"

"But—I often think how very nice he really is."

"Oh, don't say that, even in fun. I'm coming to stay with you in the summer—at the Green Gate—unless you'd rather ask Rathbone instead."

"Or unless you'd rather go yachting with the Walmers," she remarked. "They have a daughter, haven't they?"

"Oh, Valentia, be anything but blasphemous! . . ."

"Really? . . . Oh, Harry!"

"Do you mean to say you need my saying it?"

"No."

"Then, I will. Valentia, I—"

She got up and opened the door so that Daphne should not have to ring when she returned.

When the two sisters left a few minutes later, Harry sat down again as if in deep thought and lighted a cigarette. His servant came in.

"Please, sir, Mr. Van Buren is at the telephone."

"Oh well, tell him. . . Oh no—, all right—I'll go."

III

Van Buren

I t's extremely kind of you, Harry, to let me come around like this in the morning. I dare say you want to be working sometimes. I'm really afraid of being in the way, but I was rather at a loose end this morning and I wanted to have a talk with you," said Van Buren apologetically.

"Rot. Awfully glad to see you, old chap. Have a cigarette?"

"Thanks, Harry, no. I find I'm very much better if I don't smoke till after tea. . . We're intimate friends now, and yet you never call me anything but my surname, or 'old chap'. That reminds me, there's a little request I'd like to make of you, Harry."

"What's that?"

"Call me Matthew—no, call me plain Mat. It would give me real pleasure."

Harry smiled rather loudly—

"My dear fellow, I couldn't call you plain Mat. It wouldn't be suitable! You're too good-looking!"

Van Buren smiled and shook his head. In its way it was a handsome head in the fair, clean-shaven American style, with shining blond hair. He had very broad shoulders, and a very thin waist, and that naïve worldliness of air so captivating in many of his countrymen.

Except that he wore a buttonhole of Parma violets, he was dressed in every particular exactly like Harry. But no one would have believed it—he looked so much better dressed.

"That's your chaff, Harry. I'm not a Gibson man, and I don't pretend to be."

He looked at his hands, which were small and white, the finger-tips brilliantly polished, and said meditatively—

"I'm very much looking forward to meeting your cousin, Harry. I expect she's the ideal of a young English lady. Dark, did you say?"

"Rather dark, and very pretty."

"It's a curious thing, Harry, that to me a broonette has always more fascination than a blonde. It seems—I may be wrong—as though there's more piquancy, more character."

"I quite agree with you," said Harry. "Now the sister—the married one—is very fair."

"And she's quite what you call a professional beauty, isn't she?" asked Van Buren with great relish.

"My dear fellow, I don't call anyone a professional beauty, and you mustn't either. There's no such thing. I can't think how in America you get hold of these prehistoric phrases! The expression must have been dead long before either of us was born! . . . Still, she is a beauty all the same."

"Is that so? Mind you, Harry, there's something very attractive about a blonde, too. To me golden hair and blue eyes suggest gentleness and womanliness. . . What is Mrs. Wyburn like?"

"Well, she's rather like an angel on a Christmas card, with her hair down—I mean she was, as a little girl," said Harry quickly. "Now she's considered like 'Love among the Roses' by Burne-Jones."

"Do you really mean that, Harry? Why, she must be more beautiful than Miss de Freyne!"

"I wouldn't worry about her, if I were you," Harry said.

"Why not, Harry?"

"Well, you see she's got a husband," said Harry, looking at the ceiling as he puffed his cigarette.

"And a cousin," replied Van Buren with unexpected quickness. He then burst out laughing.

"What do you mean?" asked Harry, not laughing.

"Harry, I do beg of you to forgive my indiscretion. I'm afraid you'll think it shows great want of delicacy on my part. It was only meant for English chaff. Don't be angry, Harry." Van Buren was quite distressed.

"That's all right, old chap."

"You see, I know you painted her portrait, and if you *had* felt a little sentiment for her, who could blame you? Of course, I'm well aware that you're far too much a man of high principle to come any way between a woman and her husband, or even to let her know if you had a fancy in that direction. . . I thoroughly do you justice there, Harry."

"I regard them as sisters," answered Harry.

Van Buren went to the window and stood looking out for a few minutes.

"Well, they are sisters. . . What a wonderful place your London is!" he said. "Now there's the sort of thing I never can understand, which has just happened. A lady called a taxicab. Just as it came up a man—at least I suppose he calls himself a man—opened the door. I thought he meant to help her in. No! He got in himself and drove away.—Now, Harry, how do you account for that?"

"I suppose he could walk quicker," said Harry.

"It's the one fault I have to find with you Englishmen, Harry—the single fault. You're not gallant enough to the ladies. Nor is there, in my opinion, quite enough respect shown to them. I am always astonished, I admit, that they don't resent it. Why, in New York—."

"My dear fellow, they complain bitterly that there's too much respect shown to them already," said Harry. "A little more, and they'd do without us altogether!"

Van Buren laughed cheerily, and clapped Harry on the shoulder.

"What a fellow you are for chaff! Now, will you come around and have lunch with me?"

"When? Now? Thanks, old chap."

"That's real good, Harry," said Van Buren, his eyes sparkling with joy, "and we'll walk down Piccadilly together. I must say. . ."

"What?"

"I shan't feel we're real pals till you call me Mat!"

Harry shivered ostentatiously.

They went out, both laughing with great cordiality.

At the corner Van Buren stopped to throw away his buttonhole. He saw they were not being worn.

IV

THE ELDER MRS. WYBURN

Romer's mother usually received him with a sarcastic remark, such as "Oh, so you remember that I'm not dead yet?" or "I wonder you find time to come at all," or something of the same nature, calculated to cast a gloom over any visit.

The widow of a rich brewer, Mrs. Wyburn lived in a bad-tempered looking old house in Curzon Street, with a harassed footman, a domineering maid, a cross cook, and other servants that were continually changing. She was one of those excellent housekeepers who spend most of their time "giving notice" and "taking up" characters. She nearly always wore a hard-looking black silk dress. She had parted black hair, long earrings, and a knot of rare old imitation lace at her throat. Eagerness, impatience, love of teasing and sharp wit were visible in her face to one who could read between the lines. But, notwithstanding this, as she had a soft heart and plenty of hard cash, she was not altogether unpopular. People enjoyed going to hear the nasty things she said about their friends. She had a real *succès de scandale* on her Wednesdays, notwithstanding the fact that a more highly respectable lady had never existed in the world.

She adored Romer, although his slow speech and long pauses often drove her to the very verge of violence.

"Thought I'd look in," he remarked, rather heavily taking a seat in the dark drawing-room, and he proceeded by slow stages to tell her that he was coming to dinner on Thursday because Valentia was going out.

She gave him a quick look, combined of motherly pride and annoyance.

"Delighted, of course, dear. Who did you say was Valentia's hostess?"

"She's going with Daphne. Harry's dinner. At some restaurant."

"Oh, indeed! . . . Well, if you approve of these Bohemian arrangements it's not *my* business. I have my own opinion of Harry de Freyne; I always have had—and I shall keep it."

"Do," said Romer, unconsciously epigrammatic.

She waited a minute and then said—

"I don't wish to worry you, my dear. . ."

"No?"

". . . But I, personally, if I were a man. . . perhaps I oughtn't to say it—if I saw my wife so much in the society of a person like Harry de Freyne—upon my word, I should begin to ask myself what were their relations!"

"Cousins," said Romer.

He began to tap his foot slowly against the rail of the chair, but remembered Valentia's constant advice, and decided he would not quarrel.

"Well, you know your affairs best, dear. I'm only an interfering disagreeable old woman, who knows very little of modern customs and ways."

He nodded sympathetically, without answering.

"I love and admire Valentia—in many ways. She's so pretty, but not a mere doll! And we women—even the happiest of us—have to go through so much! Does she go through the housekeeping books herself, dear?" Mrs. Wyburn inquired, with dangerous sweetness.

"Shouldn't think so."

"Ah! that seems rather a pity. Still, I'm just to every one, and I will say that she's not extravagant—but has so much cleverness that she could manage very well on half the allowance you give her!"

"Is that new—that china bird?" Romer asked, getting up to look at a strange, shiny, abnormal-looking parrot on a twig that adorned the mantelpiece.

"Do you like it?" she asked.

"It seems all right. Rather jolly."

"Oh! Well, it's funny you haven't noticed it before. Considering it's been there all your life, and you used to play with it when you were four, it's odd it's escaped your notice. You played with it when you were four!" she repeated, growing rather heated.

"Did I though?"

"But things do escape your notice—that's just the point. I sometimes wish I didn't see so much myself."

"So do I," he answered. "May I smoke, mother?"

"Of course you may, dear. You may do anything on earth you like. Have some tea? *I* never have anything but China tea, so it won't do you any harm."

"I hate China tea," he answered reflectively, after what seemed to his mother about half an hour's deep thought.

. . . "But what I always have said about Valentia is that though we all admit, dear, that she has charming manners, is bright and amusing and very sweet—"

He smiled.

"*Outwardly*, is there anything behind it all? Has she any depth?" She quickly answered her own question, "*I* think she has; a great deal. I believe Valentia is extremely clever in her own way; she turns *you* round her little finger. But that wouldn't matter so much—anything's better than quarrelling and snapping and finding fault continually—which is a thing I hate. But, really, there's one point I'm quite anxious about—in fact, I often lie awake the whole night—the entire night—and wake up in the morning utterly worn out through thinking about it, Romer dear. There's nothing like a mother's heart—and this does make me anxious, I own."

"What?"

"Why, that she should ever be talked about! That she should be considered a flirt—and that sort of thing! I couldn't bear the idea of my son's wife having her name coupled with that of any young man—or any nonsense of that sort. It would be most painful to me. I'm sure I ask every one who knows her if anything of that kind is ever said."

Romer threw away the cigarette and stood up.

"What infernal rot!" he said, with a heightened colour.

Her eyes brightened with pleasure. She was delighted to have irritated him at last out of his calmness.

"Well, well, perhaps I'm a little over-anxious. It's all love, all devotion to you, dear. Of course, people do talk. There's no doubt about that; but good gracious! we all know there's nothing in it. Don't we? Don't be cross with your poor old mother, Romer."

"That's all right. I must be off. Eight on Thursday, eh?"

She kissed him affectionately, walked with him to the landing, where she kept him for about ten minutes complaining of the awful worry she had had about the under-housemaid, and of the sickening impossibility of getting a piano-tuner to attend to the instrument properly without making any sound.

"For I'm a mass of nerves, my dear. Give my best love to dear Valentia."

V

ROMER

Romer walked back, trying to throw off the irritating effect of his mother's pin-pricks. As was his usual custom when he was a little depressed, he went home and sat down in front of his wife's portrait. He often sat there for an hour when she was out, looking at it. Any one watching him would have thought he was in a state of calm and stupid content. In reality, he was worshipping. His passion for his wife was his one romance, his one interest, his one thought. He had been married five years, and had never yet expressed it in words. He was one of the unfortunate people who are not gifted with the power of expression, either in word or look. He was practically inarticulate.

As he gazed at the picture—he was feeling a little sad—the sadness melted away. The frail figure, bright yet dim, vaguely appearing through vaporous curtains, holding an impossible gold flower, had the effect on him of a beautiful Madonna on a deeply devout Catholic. It produced in him a form of religious ecstasy. He adored her with passion, and with the selfishness and jealousy of passion, but circumstances and his temperament caused it to take the outward form, principally, of care for her happiness. When she was actually present, she still dazzled him so much that he could show his feeling only by listening to and agreeing with every word she said, by doing what she asked him, and by trying to protect her, often without her knowledge, from any kind of pain or trouble. She would have been amazed had she realised the violence of his devotion to her. Apparently cool and matter-of-fact, he was in reality a reticent fanatic. He neither analysed nor showed his sentiment, nor did he himself know its extent. He wondered why certain people, certain subjects gave him pain. He trusted Valentia absolutely, nor could she in his eyes do wrong, and it was only with the subconscious second sight of love that he sometimes felt a curious and melancholy presentiment. He did not know himself that this suffering was jealousy.

What nonsense his mother talked! . . .

Harry! . . . Harry was the best fellow in the world—almost like a brother, his greatest friend, though not exactly an intimate friend.

Romer was too shy to be intimate with any one. Harry was lively, amusing, a brilliant talker; kind, good-natured, a capital chap. He appreciated Valentia, or he could not have painted that portrait. Romer was very grateful for the portrait; yet it sometimes hurt him to think Harry had painted it. It showed how well Harry understood Valentia.

This thought Romer always suppressed. He thought it was mean, and he could not be mean.

He looked out of the window. It was raining—a chilly spring shower—but there was a stir in the air, a rattle in the town, a sense of something that was going to happen; summer was not far off, and in the summer, at the end of the season, they would go down to the Green Gate, the lovely country house with the dream garden as Valentia called it, all built, planted, and arranged on purpose for her. Valentia was more herself at the Green Gate than anywhere else. Leisure suited her, and roses.

Every year Romer silently counted the weeks until they went back there. It was where he was happiest. Of course, they were not alone. Dear little Daphne was always with them, dear little thing (she was nearly six feet high)—and other people, very often, and Harry—always Harry. Perhaps Daphne would marry soon, but what about Harry?

Romer felt rather wearied when he remembered Valentia had said Harry was made to be a bachelor. Was he tired of Harry? Not a bit! Harry was a capital chap; besides, he didn't see so very much of him in London.

Heaps of people admired Valentia, and that did not annoy Romer at all (though it did not please him particularly), but he knew, again subconsciously, that Valentia cared less than nothing for any admirers, but she certainly was awfully fond of Harry. And no wonder! Harry was the best fellow in the world—lively, amusing, quite a brilliant talker; kind, good natured, and he appreciated Valentia, or he could not have painted that portrait. . .

Round and round the same thoughts passed through his brain.

It was raining—a chilly spring shower. Had Valentia got her wrap with her?

He got up, went into the hall, and saw her fur cloak hanging on a peg.

She evidently didn't care for it. She was tired of it—perhaps it was out of fashion; if so, she would never wear it. She might catch cold.

He was not a prompt man, but he went at once to the telephone and gave orders to a shop in Bond Street that would result in a collection of fur-lined cloaks being sent for her choice that evening. This would please her; she would smile and try them on. Besides, it would prevent her catching cold.

VI

HARRY'S ENTERTAINMENT

V an Buren, who was a business man, was an idealist; while Harry de Freyne, the artist—was, emphatically, not.

Van Buren had been brought up on Thackeray and Dickens, above all on old pictures from *Punch*; Du Maurier's drawings enjoyed at an early age had made him romantic about everything connected with London. As soon as he was able to leave his bank in New York—in fact, the moment he had retired from business—he had realised his dream and come to live in London. And Harry seemed to him the incarnation of everything delightfully, amusingly English. He had a real hero-worship for Harry, who was so astonishingly clever as well. Van Buren was not a snobbish Anglomaniac, at least his snobbishness was not of the common quality nor about the obvious things; he was a little ashamed of his money, but he did not worship rank and titles; it was Intellect—but Intellect that had the stamp of fashion—that held a glamour for him. So did everything that he supposed to be modern, previous, and up-to-date. No one could ever, whether in New York or in London, have been in life less modern than poor Van Buren, though he was eminently contemporary and perhaps even in advance in matters connected with business. For business he had genius, and yet, curiously, no passion; he was unconsciously brilliant on the subject; it was hereditary. But in his innermost heart he believed that it was vulgar to be an American millionaire! And he had a childish horror of vulgarity, and an innocent belief that an Englishman who had been to Eton and Oxford and who was *dans le mouvement*, smart and good-looking, and had deserted diplomacy for art, must of necessity be refined, superior, cultured, everything that Van Buren wanted to be.

Of course he soon found out that Harry was frightfully hard up, and in the most delicate manner imaginable—a delicacy rather wasted on his friend—implored, as a special favour, to be allowed to be his banker. But Harry had refused, having vague ideas of much more important extent than a mere loan with regard to making Van Buren useful. He had thus gone up in his friend's estimation, at the same time placing him under a great and deeply felt obligation by gratifying his fancy for knowing clever people and celebrities.

At last the friendship had culminated in Harry's suggestion of a marriage between his young cousin, Daphne, and Van Buren. Harry felt that if he could compass this arrangement he would at one stroke give fortune to Daphne, freedom to himself—the child was very much in his way in Valentia's house—and make Van Buren eternally grateful.

Harry really liked Van Buren and respected him; he regarded him as touching, but also, at times, as a menace. A shadow sometimes came over their friendship, the alarming shadow of the future bore. What was now to his cynical mind screamingly funny about the American— his sensitive delicate feelings, his high standard of morals with regard to what he called the ladies, and illusions that one would rarely find in London in a girl of seventeen, might some day develop into priggishness and tediousness, and—especially—would take up too much time. For since Harry had been intimate with Van Buren he had discovered that the tradition of American hustling was, like most traditions, a fiction. Americans always have time; Englishmen never. The leisurely way in which Van Buren talked was an example of this—it was the way he thought; his brain worked slowly. Harry and his like have no time to drawl; they have to keep appointments.

On the evening of the Ritz dinner-party Harry was not in a particularly good temper, and thought to himself he was rather like a Barnum as he introduced his guests one by one to the modest millionaire, who said to them all, "Pleased to meet you", and fixed his admiring glance with a sentimental respect on Daphne, an undisguised admiration on Valentia, and an almost morbid curiosity on Miss Luscombe, the first actress he had ever met.

Miss Luscombe was a conventional, rather untidy-looking creature, very handsome, with loose hair parted and waved over her ears, and with apparently no design or idea either in her dress or manner. She varied from minute to minute from being what she thought theatrical to appearing what she supposed to be social. She evidently hadn't settled on her pose, always a disastrous moment for a natural woman who wishes to be artificial. Practically she always wore evening dress except in the evening, so while at her own flat in the afternoon she was photographed in a *décolletée* tea-gown, this evening she was dressed as if for Ascot, except for the hat, with an emaciated feather boa and a tired embroidered *crêpe de Chine* scarf thrown over her shoulders, also a fan, long gloves, and a rose in her hair by way of hedging. To these ornaments she added a cold, of which she complained as soon as she saw the other guests. But no one listened. No one ever listened to Miss Luscombe, no one ever could, and yet in a way she was popular—a kind of pet among a rather large circle of people. Women never disliked her because she created no jealousy and always unconsciously put herself at a disadvantage; men did not mind her prattle and coquettish airs, being well aware that nothing was expected of them. For Miss Luscombe, though vain, was a pessimist, and quite good-natured. She was also a standing joke.

The other guests besides Valentia in yellow and Daphne in pink—both looking as fresh as daisies and as civilised as orchids—consisted of Lady Walmer, a smart, good-looking, commonplace woman, rather fatter than she wished to be, but very straight-fronted, straightforward, and sporting, with dark red hair and splendid jewels; a faded yet powerful beauty who had been admired in the eighties, but had only had real success since she turned forty-six.

With her was her daughter, a girl who at the first glance looked eight feet high, but who really was not very much above the average length. She was a splendid athlete, and her talk was principally of hockey. She wore a very smart white dress and had a dark brown neck, pretty fair hair, and an entirely unaffected bonhomie that quite carried off the harshness of her want of style or charm—in fact it had a charm of its own. Besides, it was well known that her grandmother had left her an estate in the country and £ 7000 a year, and that Lady Walmer was anxious to get her married. Hence Miss Walmer never wanted for partners at balls nor for attention anywhere, but—it was always for *le bon motif*. As Valentia said, she was the sort of girl (poor girl!) that one could only marry.

Hereford Vaughan, who was an object of considerable curiosity to several of the guests on account of his phenomenal success in having eleven plays at the same time being performed in London, New York, Berlin, Paris, and every other European city, was, to those who did not know him before, an agreeable surprise. Heaven knows what exactly people expected of him; perhaps the men feared 'side' and the women that he would be overpowering after so many triumphs, but he was merely a rather pale, dark, and rather handsome young man. He behaved like anybody else, except that perhaps his manner was a little quieter than the average. Unless one was very observant (which one isn't), or unless one listened to what he said, he did not at first appear too alarmingly clever. He had one or two characteristics which must have at times led to misunderstandings. One was that whatever or whoever he looked at, his dark opaque eyes were so full of vivid expression that women often mistook for admiration what was often merely observation. For instance, when he glanced at Lady Walmer she at once became quite confused, and intensely flattered, nearly blushed and asked him to dinner. While, if she had but known, behind that dark glance was merely the thought, "So that's the woman that Royalty. . . What extraordinary taste!"

Hereford Vaughan, who was himself thirty-four, did not share in the modern taste for the battered as a charm in itself, though he could forgive it—or, indeed, anything else—if he were amused.

Knowing that Miss Luscombe, hoping for a part, would be painfully nice to Vaughan, Harry had good-naturedly placed them as far apart as possible. Nevertheless she leaned across the table and said—

"How *do* you think of all these clever things, Mr. Vaughan? I can't think how you do it!"

"Yes, indeed, we'd all like to know that," said Captain Foster, the baby Guardsman, as Valentia called him. He spoke enviously. He was a perfectly beautiful blond, delightfully stupid, and had been longing for enough money to marry somebody ever since he was seventeen.

"I'm sure I'd jolly soon write a play if I only knew how."

"It's perfectly easy, really," said Vaughan; "it's just a knack."

"Is it though?"

"That's all."

"How do you get the things taken?"

"Oh, that's a mere fluke—a bit of luck," said Vaughan.

Every one who heard this sighed with relief to think that was how he regarded it.

Vaughan always used this exaggerated modesty as an armour against envy, for envy, as a rule, is of success rather than of merit. No one would have objected to his talent deserving recognition—only to his getting it.

"Now what do you think of Miss Luscombe?" Valentia asked the dramatist.

"I don't think of her. I never regard people on the stage as real people," Vaughan answered.

"Don't you, really? Well, you ought to know. You have made a sort of corner in 'leading ladies'. What curious clothes she wears!"

"Doesn't she? On the stage she dresses like an actress, and off the stage she doesn't dress like a lady. She's so extraordinarily vague," he said.

"Yes; and yet I've heard that, though she's so dreamy and romantic, she's quite wonderfully practical, really. She never accepts an engagement unless she gets a large salary—and all that sort of thing."

"I see. She lives in the clouds, but she insists on their having a silver lining," said Vaughan. "Who's the pink young man she's confiding in now?"

"It's Mr. Rathbone. He likes theatres—at least he collects programmes and posters, I think. Besides, he's tattooed."

"Oh, yes. That must be a great help in listening to Miss Luscombe. He's been trained to suffer."

Miss Luscombe was talking rather loudly and most confidentially to Rathbone, who had an expression of willing—but agonised—martyrdom on his fair pink, clean-shaven features.

"I *told* dear George Alexander that I would have been only *too* pleased to understudy Irene in the new piece—in fact, it would have just suited me, Mr. Rathbone, and left me plenty of time for my social engagements too. Besides, if I once got a chance of a part like that I feel I should have made a hit. Oh, it was a cruel disappointment! After being too charming to me—or, at any rate, I was charming to him at the Cashmores' reception, you know—I remember he was standing in the refreshment-room with Mrs. Cashmore, and I went *straight* up to him and said, 'Don't you remember me, Mr. Alexander?'—and after all this he only promised me—and that conditionally—a horrid, silly little part in the curtain-raiser in No. 2 B Company on tour. On tour! Of course I refused that—one must keep up one's prestige, Mr. Rathbone. There's a great deal of injustice in the profession. Talent counts for nothing—it's all influence. But I've always had a great ambition ever since I was a little girl." Miss Luscombe put her head on one side and talked as she had to the interviewer of *The Perfect Lady*. "It was always my dream—do you know?—to marry a great actor—or, at any rate, to be his great friend—like Irving and Ellen Terry—that sort of thing—a great, lifelong friendship! And as a child I was madly in love with the elder George Grossmith, but I don't think he ever knew it. Too bad!"

She pouted childishly, gave her arch musical laugh with its three soprano notes and upward inflection, and then accepted a quail with a heavy sigh.

"When I was a boy," said Rathbone in a low concentrated voice of reminiscence—he spoke rather quickly, for he had been trying in vain during the whole of dinner to get a word in edgeways and feared to lose his chance now—"when I was a boy I was in love, too, with some one on the stage. Between ourselves—you won't mention it, will you, Miss Luscombe?—"

"You can trust me," she said earnestly, with a look of Julia Neilson.

"Good! Well, I was in love, and I've got her initials—C. L.—tattooed on me now!"

"Impossible! How exciting! Who is C. L.?"

He looked round the table and murmured in a low voice, "Cissie Loftus. Isn't it odd? I wrote and told her about it, but I never received an answer to my letter."

"Poor, poor boy! I call that really touching! Will you show me the initials some day?"

"Oh no. Impossible." He was stern, adamantine. She hastily went on. "So you're very keen—interested in the stage, Mr. Rathbone?"

"Well, in the stage door. I collect programmes, and I haven't missed a first night since I was twenty!"

"Fancy! Then I ought to remember your face, at all the theatres!"

"I mean at the Gaiety," he said, "only the Gaiety."

"Oh, the Gaiety!" she turned her shoulder to him.

"Yes, Miss Daphne, if you would come out to New York you'd have a real good time. You'd turn all the young fellow's heads. I'm afraid you'd do a terrible amount of damage there. I should like to show you and Mrs. Wyburn Newport in the season, too. You ladies have it all your own way over the other side of—may I say, the herringpond?"

"Oh, please do; yes, *do* say the herringpond!"

Daphne leant forward and said to Harry:

"Do you know who is that very distinguished-looking man who has just come in—rather weary and a little grey on the temples? He bowed and kissed the woman's hand so charmingly—at the next table to us. Looks like a great diplomatist."

"Then he must be a stockbroker," said Valentia decidedly. "Every one with the grand manner always is."

"Really! I can't say; I don't know any stockbrokers," said Miss Luscombe.

"How distinguished that sounds!" murmured Vaughan.

"It's very clever of you, Miss Luscombe," said Lady Walmer; "I don't see how you can help it! I know nobody else. I always tell Alec she'll have to marry one, and when she says she doesn't want to, 'My dear child,' I say, 'you can't marry people you don't see!' And almost the only people she ever sees at our house *are* stockbrokers—except a few soldiers who never have a penny."

Alec was the daughter, named after her distinguished godmother.

"It's quite gone out to be snobbish now," Lady Walmer continued in a lower voice to Harry. "We're all only too glad to take all we can get in exchange for anything we give!"

"And you don't call that snobbish?" said Harry.

"My dear, no!—of course, we give as little as possible. I talk like this and yet I married for love—and you know the result! Walmer's always gambling, always running after—goodness knows what—and leaves me—not quite in the gutter, but certainly on the kerb!"

"Don't you want Alec to marry for love?"

"I'm afraid she'll have to, my dear—she's not very attractive. It's a blessing she's an heiress. But if she's allowed to play hockey, and skate, and fence, and dance, and the husband is fairly kind to her, I'm sure she'll be happy—I mean, I have no idea of her marrying a duke, Harry. I shall be satisfied if he's a charming man, and not too selfish." She lowered her voice still more to add—"You know she likes you, poor child, don't you?"

"You're making fun of me, dear Lady Walmer."

"No, I'm not. . . Walmer's taken 'Flying Fish' again, and after Cowes we're going for a long cruise. You must come with us. Her father will be all right. He lets me have my own way about her. Well, aren't you coming?"

"You're too frightfully kind, Lady Walmer, of course. But—"

"My dear boy, of course you're going to the Green Gate, but I wish you'd listen to a woman of the world. That," she gave Valentia a piercing glance, "can't go on for ever! You will find Romer making a row some day, and that will be a bore for you. He's just the sort of man who would."

Valentia, noticing their confidential tone and feeling instinctively that some treachery was in the air, looked once angrily at Harry and then became apparently absorbed in the conversation of Vaughan.

Every one was talking volubly and gaily. Only Daphne and Captain Foster were silent as they sat side by side looking at their plates. But they were the only people who had found the dinner a real success.

Harry, who with all his *usage du monde* was peculiarly subject to sudden obscure impulses as of the primitive man, became pale with a strange and painful sensation as he looked at Valentia.

She was flirting with Vaughan, or so every one present must be thinking. Of course it was only from pique, and he would soon put a stop to it.

And Vaughan, with his ironical glance and quiet manner, why did he look into her eyes all the time?

What was he saying?

Harry asked them all to come back to the studio for some music, but even as he made the arrangement to drive Valentia, he remembered that, *à la fin des fins*, he would have to leave her at her husband's house. Would Romer be sitting up? What an ass he was! What rot the whole dinner was! It was all through Van Buren. Van Buren was a fool. Confound Romer!

Harry was jealous.

VII

DAPHNE

More flowers from Van Buren? Let me look at them. A spray of lilies of the valley; how touching! He expects you to wear them at the opera. I think it's *such* a mistake to wear real flowers on an evening dress. They have a damp, chilly look, like fresh vegetables, at first, and when they begin to fade they make you look faded, too. Never mind, Daphne; I think perhaps you'd better wear them just tonight," said Valentia.

"Yesterday," said Daphne, "he sent me that basket of American Beauty roses. The day before he sent me Ella Wheeler Wilcox's poems."

Valentia smiled. "Poor darling!—I mean Van Buren's a poor darling, not you. You see, he's got the nice sort of Boston idea that a man ought only to send a girl flowers or books, or music. He thinks it's respectful. But, anyway, it's a very good sign."

"A good sign? But I thought there was so much of that sort of thing—I mean fuss and attention, to girls in America. I thought that didn't mean anything. I mean anything particular."

"Daphne, dear, don't blind yourself; don't shut your eyes to obvious facts. It isn't a matter of what you think or what I think, or of speculation at all. I *happen to know* that Van Buren *is* going to propose to you. He'll probably do it at Henley or at Sandown, or in the Park. He's certain to want it to be on a typically English background; but you can take it from me, for a dead cert, that it's bound to come."

Daphne sat down and looked serious.

"Valentia, it's no good. Don't let him do it. It will be so frightfully uncomfortable meeting him afterwards."

"Frightfully uncomfortable meeting the man to whom you're engaged? Why?"

"Because I shan't be engaged to him."

"Why not?"

"I shall never marry, Valentia."

Valentia stared at her in silence.

"What is your idea, darling? Why, you won't be eighteen till June. You can't be sure you'll never want to marry!"

"Well, I don't care for Van Buren."

"I thought you liked him so much?"

"Well, he seems all right at first. But I simply couldn't stand him always about."

"Couldn't you? Poor pet! But he mightn't *be* always about."

"Well, I couldn't stand his marked attention. Valentia, I *hate* marked attention."

"Do you, really? Who'd have thought it?"

"Well—and he'd always be so considerate and so thoughtful and so respectful!"

"That mightn't last when you were married," said Valentia consolingly.

"Perhaps he might not be so bad after we were once married. . . But I shouldn't like to risk it. And the engagement! Oh! I couldn't simply *stand* the engagement! Just think of the ring, and the sentiment, and the fuss, and the letters! Oh, he'd enjoy it all so much! Oh, it would make me simply sick to see how pleased he'd be!"

"I know that feeling," said Valentia sympathetically, nodding her head.

"Oh, and don't you see how he'd think he was engaged to a well-brought-up, nice English girl who was a relation of Harry's, and knew all the right people, and all that sort of thing? And he'd take a big house—he's hinted this to me already—most likely in Park Lane—anyhow, something just like a millionaire in a book. It's all so dull, and cut-and-dried."

"Some of these cut-and-dried obvious things turn out quite jolly afterwards. It's the uncomfortable, romantic things that are more often failures. And you know, Daphne, you do like pretty things and clothes, and going everywhere, and—not only that, he's really such a dear, and a good sort, and so good-looking! And you'd put me into a very awkward position with Harry if you refuse him. But, of course, darling, you must do as you like."

"Well, then, Valentia, don't *let* me refuse him. I don't want to. Don't let it come to that. I'm sure I should loathe to hear him propose."

"Why?"

"It would make me sick."

"What can I tell Harry really as your reason for not being able to stand Van?"

"I'm sure *I* don't know!"

"He bores you," announced Valentia. "That's what's the matter. He doesn't amuse you."

"It isn't that, it isn't that!" cried Daphne vehemently. "I don't *want* to be amused. Do you think I like a man because he's clever, or funny, and always making jokes? That bores me frightfully. Harry's way of being lively and clever bores me to *death*! I don't want to marry a professional entertainer! No, Valentia, that's more the sort of thing you'd like. *You're* quite sorry Romer's not like that."

"I don't suggest that it would be ideal to marry Harry Lauder, Daphne dear. But wouldn't you really like someone fairly intelligent?"

"No. Why should I? Do you think I want to marry a man so horribly clever that he wouldn't understand a word I said?"

"Let's have it out, dear. What do you think you want?" Valentia answered herself; "It's Foster, of course! That dull, empty-headed, commonplace, hard-up, handsome boy. You can't marry him. He's just twenty-two, and has only a miserable allowance, and is in an expensive regiment, and you, darling, will only have three hundred a year. I should love to see you happy in your own way and having your wish, but don't you think it's a childish fancy? You're both children. Of course he hasn't suggested marriage, yet, has he? He knows perfectly well it's out of the question."

"Valentia! Darling! Why, he proposed to me the day we were introduced—at Prince's, and he's been doing it ever since."

"Oh, how utterly absurd of him! Well, anyhow, you must wait and see. Even if he could afford it, I don't think it would be a success. Why, there's nothing in the boy! What do you see in him?"

"I like the way he laughs," said Daphne, after a pause.

"Do you mind telling me one thing straight out? I'm being very nice to you about this, dear. I ought to scold you. But, at any rate, you must treat me with complete confidence."

"Of course, of course, dear."

"Tell me, he hasn't ever kissed you, has he?"

"Oh, Valentia!"

"I beg your pardon, darling. I felt sure he hadn't."

"Of course he has."

"He has!—Where?"

"How do you mean, where? Oh! at every dance where we've ever met. He always does, whenever he can. Is it so dreadful? He's such a boy!"

"Fancy your liking him enough for that!" said Valentia, stupefied.

"Oh, he's a darling; and the only person I ever could possibly marry."

"It's rather serious," said Valentia; "and poor Van who is so devoted!"

"He isn't, really," said Daphne decidedly.

"Don't you think so? Why?"

"Oh, the whole thing's an *idea*—the sort of thing he *wants to do*. It's not genuine."

"I should have thought the feelings of a man of thirty-four who could marry any one he chose would be more real than the fancy of a mere boy! Boys like anybody."

"Van isn't genuine like Cyril," said Daphne.

"Who on earth's Cyril?"

"Captain Foster."

Valentia walked round the room and then said—

"And you really suppose you're going to adore him all your life?"

"I *suppose* so. I really don't know. I know about now. Oh, Valentia, be a darling and let him come to the fancy ball with us." She kissed her. "And, oh, do tell Harry to explain to Van that it can't go on, that he must put it out of his head. Do, darling Valentia. Any well-brought-up young girl will do for him just as well!"

"And wouldn't any well-brought-up young girl do for Cyril?"

"I don't know. But only Cyril will do for me. Oh! the jolly way he has of saying 'Righto' and 'You're all right,' and calling me 'little girl!' Oh, he *is* a dear!"

"Oh, well, if he says such brilliant things as *that*!"

"It isn't what he *says*—"

"Oh, hush, Daphne, here is Romer. I shan't tell him a word about it. Well, I'll think it over." She called Daphne back and said in a half-hearted way—

"I suppose it wouldn't do just to sort of please Harry by marrying Van, and then seeing that silly boy now and then. You'd so soon get tired of him—but, no! that wouldn't be right. Forget that I said it—I don't mean it."

"I couldn't stand Van at all," said Daphne definitely, "whether I saw Cyril or not."

"Then you shan't be bothered with him. But can't you give up Cyril? I know I'm right about it. It isn't only the hard-upness and the impossibility—of course, I know he's got relations and all that—but, it's he himself. You'll get bored with him, too, in a different way."

"I like him so much *now*," pleaded Daphne.

Romer came in and Valentia merely told him at great length every word of the foregoing conversation with lavish comments by herself. Secretly Romer was bitterly disappointed when he realised that the possibility of his being left alone with his wife was more remote, but of course he agreed with Valentia, as she changed her mind a dozen times on the subject, and as usual the conversation ended in a telephone message to Harry to come round at once.

VIII

In Fancy Dress

Van Buren had had many pleasures, many gratifications since he had been in London; his dreams—the dreams inspired by Du Maurier's drawings when he was a little boy—had been very nearly realised. Perhaps the greatest triumph that he had had yet was the evening of the Artists' Fancy Ball.

He had succeeded in making up a party to go in costume. He was always making up parties, and he had for many years been obsessed by a longing to dress up.

Harry, in mockery of his passion for everything English, had advised him to go as an Ancient Briton, with a coat of blue paint. Scorning such ribald chaff, he had ordered a magnificent costume of chain armour. Greatly to his satisfaction he had persuaded Hereford Vaughan to go as Shakespeare, Valentia and Daphne respectively as Portia in scarlet and Rosalind in green.

A large party were to dine at Van Buren's rooms before the ball. Fancy dress has the effect of bringing out odd, unexpected little characteristics in people. For example, Harry, good-looking and a dandy, quite a romantic type, hated dressing up, and cared nothing whatever about his costume; while Romer, the sober and serious, enjoyed it immensely, and appeared to think his appearance of the utmost importance—almost a matter of life and death.

The women were far less self-conscious in costume than the men, and cared far less how they looked, probably because women are always more or less in fancy dress, and it was not so much of a novelty to them.

Valentia had pointed out that Shakespeare, to be quite correct, should wear ear-rings; so Vaughan called at her house on the way to Van Buren's, as she had promised to lend him some.

"He won't know how to put them on," said Daphne, drawing on her long boots. "Probably he hasn't had his ears pierced; you must go and screw them on for him."

Valentia ran down. Just as she was screwing the long coral and pearl ear-rings with rather painful energy on to the unfortunate young man's ears, the servant, with a slight expression of terror that could not be concealed, announced—

"Mrs. Wyburn."

The situation was really rather comic. Romer's mother, who was going to a dinner-party in the same street, could not forgo the pleasure of calling unexpectedly on them at half-past seven, vaguely hoping that it might be inconvenient to them, and that she would catch them in something they didn't want her to know—a true mother's instinct. But not in her wildest dreams had she expected what she saw when she entered the drawing-room—her daughter-in-law in her red mortarboard, red cloak and bands, with, apparently, her arms round the neck of a young man in purple silk stockings and jewelled embroidered gloves with rings outside them.

Mrs. Wyburn literally sank into a chair.

Valentia was perfectly equal to the occasion. She thoroughly enjoyed the baffling of Mrs. Wyburn.

"I can't think why Romer didn't tell you," she repeated several times, "that Van Buren is giving a dinner for the fancy ball!" and she rang and gave orders that her husband and sister were to come down immediately.

Romer had been four hours dressing; Daphne about ten minutes.

"I do think you ought to have a little make-up. Will you?" said Valentia to Vaughan.

"I should love to," he answered, to Mrs. Wyburn's disgust and horror, looking in the glass and taking very little notice of the indignant old lady.

"He *does* need just a touch of lip-salve and a little black under the eyes, don't you think so?" Valentia asked, caressingly, pretending to consult Mrs. Wyburn.

"I can't say, I'm sure. I've no idea what he wants," said Mrs. Wyburn with a snap.

"But don't you think it would improve him, darling?" Valentia went on, holding her head on one side and holding up her hand as if she were looking at a picture.

"Not at all," said Mrs. Wyburn.

"Then do you think his lips are red enough already?" asked Valentia.

Vaughan hastily interrupted the absurd discussion.

"The human lip is never red enough," he said decidedly; "they ought to be bright, light scarlet."

"That's just what I think. I've got some lovely scarlet stuff—the colour of sealing-wax. Shall I fetch it for you?"

"Yes, do," he said.

"But won't it look rather—"

"No; merely decent," said the young man decidedly.

"And what does Romer say to *all this?*" said Mrs. Wyburn with a forced smile and a voice trembling with uncontrollable rage.

"Oh, he likes it, darling. He loves it. No one's been so keen about their dress as Romer. I'll go and fetch him, and my roll of parchment—I had forgotten my roll of parchment."

She ran upstairs and came down saying—

"Romer won't be a minute, dear; he's awfully anxious for you to see his dress. He's just darkening his eyelashes. That's all. He's Louis XIX or something, you know."

She then deliberately and openly drew Vaughan to the window where there was still bright June daylight and painted his lips a brilliant scarlet to their mutual satisfaction and Mrs. Wyburn's unspeakable horror.

"Mad," murmured Mrs. Wyburn, half to herself, "quite mad! I shall be quite upset for the Trott-Hellyers' dinner-party. It's Dr. Trott-Hellyers' birthday. He only *lives* three doors from you" (she said this rather reproachfully), "and I dine with him *every* year on his birthday! And to think I only came in to see my son for a minute or two, because I couldn't bear to pass his door. . . his very door. . ."

"Sweet of you," said Valentia.

. . . "And then to think I should find—" She screamed suddenly.

Daphne had come in, in her green cloak, doublet and hose, and little green cap, Romer in paint and powder, patches and lace ruffles, sword and snuffbox. There was a lavish amount of rouge on his cheeks and his eyes were blacked almost to the temples.

Hearing that his mother was there he had finished the left eye rather hurriedly, the result being that he looked as if he had been fighting.

While the poor lady was trying to adjust herself to this sight, and explaining for the sixth time why she was there, and making bitter remarks about a young girl going to a ball in what she (Mrs. Wyburn) called trousers, and while Daphne kept on wrapping herself in the folds of her cloak and then undoing them again to show her nice high boots, she was still more distressed at the arrival of her *bête noire* and mortal enemy, Harry de Freyne.

Van Buren had sent his motor for them, containing Harry.

Had his name not been announced by the servant, Mrs. Wyburn would certainly not have recognised Harry. He was a pierrot in white satin, with a violet tulle ruffle round his neck and a black velvet mask. One would know him solely by his single eye-glass, his pleasant voice, and fluent conversation.

Pretending to be a clown he jumped in, bowed low to Mrs. Wyburn, and kissed first Daphne and then Valentia.

With a last-straw expression Mrs. Wyburn drew herself up to her full height.

"Give me my cloak, Romer. I must go. No, don't come to the carriage with me. Suppose the Trott-Hellyers were to see you—they'd never get over it!"

"Why, it's all right, mother," Romer answered. "I'm all right. I'm a courtier—of the tenth century—you know. I'm all right."

"And you approve of your young sister-in-law going to a public ball dressed up as a man?"

"Rosalind wasn't a man, mother. You forget; you must read the *Midsummer Night's Dream* again. You've forgotten it."

"I shan't find Rosalind there. But that's not the point. When I came in I found Valentia with that man—the man who writes in purple knickerbockers—"

"No, he doesn't—he never writes in purple knickerbockers."

"Is this meant to be witty?" she asked with a freezing glare.

"What? No, I shouldn't think so."

"I found *your wife*," she said in a low hissing voice, as they passed through the hall where there was a large looking-glass—Romer's attention wandered—"within an inch of that young man's face, putting ear-rings in his ears!"

"Well, she couldn't put them in a mile off," said Romer absently.

He was now frankly turning his back on his mother, and staring at his face in the glass.

"Hang it all! I don't look so bad, do I?"

"You look a gentleman," she answered coldly; "any son of mine must look a gentleman. Of course, you look ridiculous—and, as far as that goes, you *are* ridiculous; but that doesn't matter quite so much as long as you look a gentleman."

"Oh, rot!"

Romer was trying to move a patch from one corner of his eye to the other.

"But as to Harry de Freyne? . . . And shall you allow your wife to dance with him in that costume?"

"Of course—why not? And—*doesn't* Valentia look—jolly?"

"I think the scarlet with her golden hair is rather too—striking," she answered spitefully.

"Oh, *she's* all right!"

"I think you're all mad!" she answered as she reached the door.

The servant opened it.

"Oh, we're all right. Good night, mother. You'll be late for the Trott-Hellyers."

Drawing her cloak over her narrow shoulders, Mrs. Wyburn stepped angrily into the brougham.

Although it was only three doors from her son's house, she would not for the world have walked.

When she arrived there, still in a very bad temper at all she had seen, she nevertheless boasted to her neighbour about how remarkably distinguished and handsome her son and daughter-in-law had looked in costume, and of their success, charm, perfect domestic happiness, and importance and perfection generally.

She succeeded in depressing the fossils on both sides of her, but they smiled at each other, indulgent to the feminine weakness of so amiable and devoted a mother.

IX

A Celebrity at Home

M iss Luscombe lived with her mother in a species of tank, or rather in a flat that gave that impression because it was in the basement. It was dark, and such glimpses as they had of people passing on the pavement were extremely odd; it seemed a procession of legs and skirts, like something in a pantomime or a cinematograph.

The Luscombes lived, as it were, beneath the surface; but that did not prevent their being very much *dans le mouvement*, and coming up with great frequency to the surface to breathe. And when one had once walked down the steps and found one's way into the tank, it was an extremely pleasant one, and quite artistic. It seemed original, too. There was something almost freakish in being answered by the parlourmaid (who was suitably like a fish in manner and profile), "Miss Luscombe is at home, and will you please step downstairs?" when one had rung the bell on the ground floor. And Miss Luscombe's ringing laugh with its three soprano notes and upward cadence always greeted one charmingly and cordially, and one always liked her; one couldn't help it. Her great fault was that she was never alone. She existed in an atmosphere of teaparties and 'afternoons'; like the Lotus-Eaters, she lived in 'that land where it was always afternoon'.

For an obscure person she led a singularly public life. In her existence there seemed no secrets, no shadows, no contrasts, and no domesticity. One could never imagine her except in what she regarded as full dress, nor without, by her side, a perpetual bamboo table with three little shelves in it, in which were distributed small cut pieces of very yellow cake with very black currants, sandwiches, made of rather warm thin bread and butter, pink and white cocoanut biscuits, and constant relays of strong dark tea made in a drab china teapot. On crowded afternoons—in fact, every other Thursday—little coffee cups containing lumpy iced coffee were also handed round. When they had music there were lemonade, mustard and cress sandwiches, and a buffet.

Even when Miss Luscombe was entirely alone she did not seem so. She had got into the habit of talking always as if she were surrounded by crowds, and said so much about the celebrities who ought to have turned up that one felt almost as depressed as if they had really been there. Sometimes they came, for there was no one like Miss Luscombe for firmness. Also, she was never offended and was hospitality itself, and she had a way of greeting one that was a reward for all one's trouble—it seemed much more trouble than it really was, somehow, just to step down into the tank. And she was so charming no one could help being flattered till the next visitor arrived, when she was even more charming.

After the Fancy Ball she had got hold of Valentia, who came to see her on one of those Thursdays that she had pointed out as peculiarly her own—one of *my* Thursdays. She really believed that for any one else to receive on that day was a kind of infringement of copyright.

Miss Luscombe was wearing on this occasion a drab taffeta silk dress with transparent sleeves and a low neck. She wore a rose in her hair, a necklace, and long gloves, because she said she wouldn't have time to dress again before going out to dinner.

About a dozen people were there—vague shamefaced young men with nothing to say, and confident, satirical, fluent young men with a great deal to laugh at. Most of the older women seemed a shade patronising in tone, and looked as if they had never been there before. On the faces of the young women and the girls could be read the resolution never to go there again.

Mrs. Luscombe, the mother, was so refined that there was scarcely anything of her; her presence was barely perceptible. She had learnt the art of self-effacement to the point of showing no trace of being there at all. To add to the effect of not being noticeable, she wore a dress exactly the same colour as the sofa on which she sat—like those insects who, when hiding from their foes, become the colour of the leaves on which they live. She was practically invisible.

On the other hand, Miss Luscombe herself was very much there— very much *en évidence*. Smiling, greeting, archly laughing, sweetly pouting; coquetting, eating, playing, singing, acting—almost dancing— an ideal and delightful hostess.

She said to every one as they arrived how sweet it was of them to come so early, or how naughty it was of them to come so late, or how horrid it was of them not to come last time, or how dear it would be of them if they came next. She always introduced people to each other who were not on speaking terms, and had intentionally cut each other for years. She had a real genius for making people accidentally meet who had just broken off their engagement, or had some other awkward reason for not wishing to see each other—and then pushing them together so that they could not get away. At heart she was intensely a peacemaker, but people who had met there rarely made up their quarrels.

When the favourite actor arrived she introduced him to every one till he was ready to drop, and when the great singer telegraphed he couldn't come, she showed the wire to everybody. Most of the guests preferred his not coming. Very few could have endured her triumph had he really arrived. On the other hand, they would themselves have far preferred to receive a telegram of refusal rather than not to hear from him at all.

When these entertainments were over and the mother and daughter were left alone, the daughter became far more thoroughly artificial than she was when surrounded by her friends. There was no throwing off the mask; on the contrary, it was fixed more firmly on, and Miss Luscombe gave free vent to her sham passion for imitation comedy.

On this particular Thursday, as soon as Flora Luscombe had laughed her last visitor archly to the door, she knelt by her mother's side, put her arms round her, and said—

"Dear, dear Mummy, how sweet it is to be alone!"

Mrs. Luscombe shrank back a little. This pet name, only too appropriate, always got a little on her nerves, but she felt bound to play up in an amateurish sort of way to a certain extent.

"Hadn't you better go and take off that beautiful dress?" she said. "You're not really dining out, are you?"

"No, dearest, I managed to get out of it, but alas! I've got to go to the Reception—you know—that horrid Royal Institution of Water Colours—afterwards. It isn't worth while to change again. Oh, how weary one does get of the continual round! And then tomorrow!" She sighed.

"What is it tomorrow?"

"Tomorrow! Don't talk of it! There's Mrs. Morris's At Home in Maida Hill, and then right at the other end of London the Hyslop-Dunn's in Victoria Grove. Oh, dear! And yet one feels one must be *seen* at all these places, darling, or else it's remarked at once."

"You live too much for the world," replied her mother, tidying up some half-finished watercress sandwiches with a sharp knife. She wondered if, thus repaired, they would do for next Thursday.

"You know, Mummy dear, that's the worst of our terrible profession. We must keep before the public, or else we drop out and are forgotten.

What a sweet creature Valentia Wyburn is! I thought she was quite, quite dear. And the husband and the cousin are darlings too. Of course they wouldn't come; I couldn't get them to an afternoon."

She got up and looked in the glass.

"What a crowd there was today! Three people came up to the front door at the same time. I think they enjoyed themselves, don't you? Though I feel I can't pay every one proper attention when there's such a crush, but I do my little best. . . Mr. Simpson came up to me and told me I looked quite wonderful. But he's a silly thing." She pouted and put her head on one side. "Did I look too hideous, darling?"

"Beautiful, of course. The only thing is. . ."

Miss Luscombe clapped her hands and laughed.

"Did its little girlie really look as nice as all that? Oh, Mummy, Mummy!"

"Charming, dear, I only wish that. . ."

"It's too proud of its little daughter, that's what it is," said Miss Luscombe, sitting on the arm of her mother's chair. "It's a silly, vain, conceited mother, that it is. It can't see any fault in its pet."

She tried to pat her mother's cheek. Mrs. Luscombe moved aside with justifiable irritation.

"Don't do that, Flora! Yes, dear, of course, I think you're wonderful, and looked sweet today; but I do wish. . ."

"No, no, it doesn't want anything," said Flora.

"I should be so pleased—if you'd put on just a little less lip-salve and not quite so much of that bluish powder."

Having succeeded in completing her sentence, her mother got up and faded quickly out of the room and shut the door, leaving Flora looking quite surprised and rather upset with being found fault with.

Indeed, she did not quite recover her equanimity until she had looked over the cards in the hall and put on a great deal more powder and lip-salve, after which she told her mother perhaps she was right, and in any case she, Flora, would always do what she asked, and would always follow her dear, dear Mummy's advice.

She was so charming and amiable that Mrs. Luscombe pretended to believe her, and said it was *sweet* of her to take it all off and go out that evening without any adventitious aids to beauty; and this she said in spite of the obvious fact that Flora had evidently put on considerably more than usual.

X

MISCHIEF

The elder Mrs. Wyburn was seated at the gloomy window of her sulky-looking house in Curzon Street one bright day in the season, looking out with some anxiety.

"Of course she's late; but if that woman doesn't come I'll never forgive her. She's a silly fool, but at least she does hear what's going on," she reflected.

At this moment an old-fashioned-looking victoria drove up, drawn by two large grey horses. In it sat a rather fat and important-looking lady, with greyish red hair, a straight decided mouth, and several firm chins. Her most marked characteristic was her intense decision on trivialities. She was always curiously definite on the vaguest of subjects, and extraordinarily firm and sensible about nothing in particular.

Miss Westbury was a rich unmarried woman, with a peculiarly matronly appearance, a good-natured love of giving advice, and with views that obviously dated—one did not know exactly from when. If she had some of the Victorian severities of the sixties, she had also many of the sentimental vagaries of the eighties. The serious business of her life was gossip. In her lighter moments she collected autographs. But her gossip differed from that of the nervous, impatient Mrs. Wyburn in that it was far more pompous and moral, and not nearly so spiteful and accurate.

Miss Westbury sailed in—I need hardly say she was dressed in heliotrope—and sat down rather seriously in a large—and the only comfortable—armchair.

"My dear Millie, how extremely good of you to come!" exclaimed Mrs. Wyburn.

Miss Westbury had been christened Maria, but Millie was the name which she had chosen to be called by her friends.

"I am very pleased to come, dear Isabella. To call on you on one of your Wednesdays is, I know, quite hopeless if one has anything to say. To call on any one on a day at home, except as a mere matter of form, I do not consider sensible."

"Quite so. Will you have some tea?"

Mrs. Wyburn rang the bell rather fretfully. She did not care for Millie's made conversation, and hated her way of gaining time.

"I will have what I always have, dear Mrs. Wyburn, at five o'clock, if I may—hot water with one teaspoonful of milk, and a saccharine tablet which I bring with me. I am not a faddist, and I think all those sort of fancies about what is and what is not good for one are exceedingly foolish; but when I go in for a régime, dear, I give it a fair chance. Otherwise there is no sense in it!"

She settled herself still more sensibly and decidedly in her chair.

"I wonder," said Mrs. Wyburn nervously—one could see she was not listening, and thought Miss Westbury was merely drivelling on— "whether you will come to the point at once? It would be a great comfort if you would. I have been feeling quite anxious about your visit. I rather foolishly took some coffee after lunch, and it kept me awake the whole afternoon—either that, or my anxiety."

"If you take coffee after lunch," replied Miss Westbury, "you should take it made as I do. Two teaspoonfuls of coffee in a large breakfast-cup full of hot water, a saccharine tablet, and a teaspoonful of condensed—"

"What was it you really heard, Millie dear, about my daughter-in-law?" interrupted Mrs. Wyburn sharply.

Here the footman brought in the tea. Miss Westbury frowned, and ostentatiously changed the subject.

"Have you been to the Grafton? I was persuaded to go. I think, myself, there's a great deal too much fuss made about pictures nowadays. When one thinks of the money that's wasted on them, when it might be sent to a hospital, it makes one's blood boil! And some of those that are made the most fuss about—both the Old Masters and the very new ones—these post-men, or whatever they're called—seem to me perfect nonsense. A daub and a splash—no real trouble taken—and then you're expected to rave about it. There's one man—some one wants me to buy a picture of his—he paints all his pictures in tiny squares of different colours; when you're close you can't see anything, but it seems that if you walk five feet away it forms into a kind of pattern. It seems it's the tessellated school, and they tell me that in a few years nothing else will count. And what I thought was a mountain in a mist turns out to be 'A Nun with cows grazing.' Silly nonsense I call it!"

"Was the nun grazing, or the cows?" asked Mrs. Wyburn.

ADA LEVERSON

"Goodness knows, dear. Then there was that other one called Waning Day, or something. Two people in a boat sailing on dry land! Then that picture of a purple man with a green beard! Oh, my dear! The people who took me there told me it was full of—something French— *essayage*, or *mouvement*, I think. The man who tried to make me buy it said it was symbolical. But of course I refused. You know I never have anything to do with nonsense. Well now, my dear—" Taking pity on Mrs. Wyburn's extreme impatience, Miss Westbury came a little nearer. "What I heard was simply this. My cousin, Jane Totness, took her little boy, who is in London for the holidays, to the British Museum. She always likes to improve his mind as much as possible; besides, he had been promised a treat after having a tooth out; the first week of the holidays he always has a tooth out and a treat after. Jane is like that; she's a sensible woman, and I must say I think she brings her boys up very well. I myself might have been more inclined to take him to Madame Tussaud's, or even to a matinée, or to have an ice at Buzzard's; but I dare say I'm old-fashioned enough in some ways, and Jane knows her own business best."

"No doubt she does," said Mrs. Wyburn, quivering with impatience, tapping her foot on the floor, and trying to restrain herself. "And so she took the little boy—Charlie, isn't it?—to the British Museum? Go on, dear!"

"Not Charlie, Mrs. Wyburn. It was little Laurence—little Laurence. He was called Laurence after his grandfather, Lord Dorking. It's the rule in the Totness family; the second son is always called after the grandfather, the eldest son after his father, and the third son—I mean, of course, if there is one—after the mother's father. Don't you think it's a very sensible plan, dear?"

Mrs. Wyburn gave her friend first a sympathetic smile, and then a murderous glance.

"Yes. Well?"

"Oh yes. Well, she was just pointing out something to little Laurence—he's an intelligent boy, and I dare say he was enjoying it very much—when, to her great surprise, *who* should she see but Mrs. Romer Wyburn, talking away like anything on a seat with—who do you think?"

"Who?"

"That young man Harry de Freyne—her cousin, isn't it?"

"How extraordinary!" exclaimed Mrs. Wyburn. "Did they seem uncomfortable when they saw Jane?"

"Oh dear, no, my dear. They seemed most comfortable. Jane bowed to them—of course rather coldly, she says—and they smiled and nodded, and Valentia kissed her hand to Laurence. Of course, Jane was very much pained and shocked about it all. I must say her first thought, dear, was that I should tell you. Jane Totness is a thoroughly good woman—so thoughtful."

"Do you see anything so very peculiar about it?" said Mrs. Wyburn. "You know, the young man—I disapprove of him as strongly as any one can—but he's an artist, and she is his cousin, and perhaps he wanted to show her something in the British Museum?"

"My dear Mrs. Wyburn, far be it from me to look on the dark side of things, but, as Jane said, who on earth would go to the British Museum, unless they were dragged there by force, except to have a private interview?"

"But if he wanted to speak to her alone, I don't see why he shouldn't call on her."

"That's just it. If it were a simple, innocent, harmless conversation, that is what he would have done. But it was quite clear that there was something clandestine about it, and you may be quite sure Romer knew nothing of it. Besides, they are always together."

"It does look odd," said Mrs. Wyburn. "What would you advise me to do? Shall I speak to my son or my daughter-in-law about it?"

"To neither, my dear. If you speak only to your son, he will tell her, and she will get round him, and prove there's nothing in it. If you speak to her she will get round you, and say that Romer knew all about it. My advice is, if you really want to put a stop to this flirtation—I'm sure it's gossiped about—even Jane, who is the last person in the world to talk, speaks of it to every one. If I were you, I would speak to the young man himself."

"To Harry de Freyne? Yes, it's rather a good idea."

It struck Mrs. Wyburn that to do this would, perhaps, cause more annoyance than anything else. She was now anxious to get rid of Miss Westbury, who evidently had nothing more to impart. But that lady was not so easy to dispose of. She broke into a long monologue on the subject of régime, servants, and little dressmakers, occasionally returning to the subject of the British Museum, and the shocking frivolity there.

Mrs. Wyburn was just thinking of having a violent toothache or some other ill, when Miss Westbury suddenly made up her mind to depart.

As soon as she had gone Mrs. Wyburn flew to the Blue Book, looked up Harry's address, and wrote him the following note:—

Dear Mr. de Freyne,
"Probably you hardly remember me, but I have met you on two or three occasions at the house of my daughter-in-law, Mrs. Romer Wyburn. There is something I want to say to you which I hardly like to write. I should be glad if you would come and see me tomorrow afternoon at four o'clock. I shall not keep you long. You may think this a strange request, knowing you so slightly as I do, but when we meet, I am sure you will understand.

Yours truly,
ISABELLA WYBURN

Having written this note, Mrs. Wyburn felt too impatient to send it by post; she was simply longing to know that Harry was feeling uncomfortable, as he was very certain to feel when he got the letter. Although she had a great suspicion and general dislike of the Messenger Boy Service, she relented for once in their favour so far as to make use of them, and the letter was sent by hand.

She was rewarded for thus conquering her prejudice. Harry was at home, and accepted her invitation with most respectful alacrity. His manners—especially on paper—were, with old and young ladies, always equally perfect—unless he was out of temper.

Mrs. Wyburn eagerly hoped Harry would see Valentia, or somehow convey to her about the letter, because it would be sure to make her uneasy also.

THE NEXT DAY THE YOUNG man was punctual to the moment. The old lady left him alone for a few minutes in the dark, dismal drawing-room. She thought it would have a salutary effect.

She found him, when she came in, stroking the china bird, and looking at himself in the mirror above it.

He received her with such charming grace that she felt almost disconcerted, and as if she ought to apologise.

"You received my letter?" she said, rather abruptly.

"With great pleasure. That is why I am here."

He was still standing, smiling delightfully.

"Sit down," she said, with cold graciousness. "I hope you are not in a great hurry?"

"All my day belongs to you," he replied with a low bow, taking the seat she had indicated. He looked at her with soft deference under his long eyelashes.

She found what she had to say more difficult than she had expected. She spoke quietly, in a low yet rasping voice, with a sharp dignity.

"I will come straight to the point. To put it plainly, a report has reached my ears, Mr. de Freyne, which has caused me very great pain and anxiety—I mean, as a mother. And I wondered whether you—"

"As a mother? Surely, Mrs. Wyburn, nothing against Romer? I'm sure I, as one of his oldest friends. . ."

"Against Romer!" She drew herself up stiffly. "Most certainly not! There's never been a word breathed otherwise than in dear Romer's favour since he was a little boy."

Harry appeared much relieved.

"It's a great comfort to hear you say that. It's only what I was going to assure you."

"Besides, do you suppose for one moment that if I had any fault to find with my son I should send for you?"

She already had an annoying fancy that he was defeating her, laughing at her, and turning the tables.

"It seemed certainly rather strange," Harry said.

"No, indeed! When I say I was troubled as a mother, I meant it in a very different sense. What I'm afraid of is that dear Romer might be worried if he heard the report to which I refer."

"And that is? . . ."

She looked at him spitefully, yet with a reluctant admiration.

He was irritatingly good-looking, good-humoured, and at his ease, and particularly well-dressed, without appearing in the least conscious of it. She wished immensely that he had been plain, or awkward, or even out at elbows, or absurdly dandified, or looked *nouveau riche*, or something! She felt jealous of him for Romer, and, at the back of her brain, she grudgingly and perversely sympathised a little with her daughter-in-law. Harry radiated a peculiar charm for women of all ages. He did not study them nor try very much to please them; the fascination was involuntary; he simply used it.

"And that is, that you and my daughter-in-law, Valentia, were seen *alone*—" she paused a moment, showing a latent instinct for dramatic effect.

He smiled a little more, and bent his head forward with every sign of intelligent interest.

She spoke with emphasis.

"*Alone*—the other morning—at the British Museum!"

Somehow she felt the shot had missed fire. It had fallen flat. It was less effective than she had hoped. It did not sound so very shocking after all.

He continued to smile with the air of waiting for the climax. She gathered herself together and went on—

"I heard it from Miss Westbury, so it is a fact!"

Harry thought of saying that he preferred an old wives' tale any day to an old maid's fact, but he only smiled on.

"Of course, if this is untrue, Mr. de Freyne—if it is a mistake, or a false report, you have merely to deny it. Assure me it is incorrect—on your word of honour—and I will then contradict it in the proper quarter."

He decided on his line. "My dear lady, pray don't contradict it. As a report it is a gem—it is unique. Not merely because it's absolutely true—for, as a matter of fact, I think most reports are—but because of its utter unimportance! It seems to me so trivial—so dull—so wanting in interest to the general public."

"You think reports are usually true, Mr. de Freyne?"

"I am convinced they are. I believe firmly in the no-smoke-without-fire theory. Oh, do you know, I think it is *so* true! . . . This certainly is true—it's a solemn fact."

"You admit it?"

"I do indeed! Surely I could hardly refuse to go when I was asked?"

"Oh, you were asked?"

"Certainly. And Romer is really such a very old friend of mine, I could hardly refuse his request. I may be wrong, but I think one should always be ready to take a little trouble for an old friend."

"No doubt you have very strict ideas on the duties and obligations of friendship! At *his* request—my son's?"

"Yes; your son asked me to go and escort Valentia."

"It is very peculiar; you must see that your explanation sounds extremely odd."

"Not at all odd," he answered softly, "if you will allow me to contradict you." He thought a moment. Then he went on: "You may have heard, perhaps, about the dance that little American, Mrs. Newhaven, is getting up at the Grafton Galleries for *Deaf and Dumb Dogs and Cats*. No? Well, every one is going, and they're arranging to have, by way of novelty, Quadrilles of different nationalities. Romer and his wife are to dance in the Egyptian Quadrille, and he asked me to take her to the British Museum to look round and see if we could find some inspiration for Egyptian costumes that wouldn't be too impossible. But when we got there, we suddenly remembered the awful story about one of the mummies being unlucky, so we went into the Print Room and remained there."

De Freyne paused.

"Of course, if that is all—if my son knows of your going, and even asked you to go, there's nothing more to be said. . . though I think it very foolish, and I don't approve of any of that sort of thing at all."

"What, not of Egyptian quadrilles, Mrs. Wyburn?" asked Harry, with surprised innocence and in a coaxing voice. "Why, I'm sure it will be frightfully harmless—in fact, very invigorating to the mind. It's not as though the dresses were becoming! We saw the most hideous things at the Museum. We met Lady Totness, who was dragging a wretched little boy about—I suppose as a punishment for something."

Mrs. Wyburn smiled slightly. She began to feel rather inclined to relent at the implication that Lady Totness was hideous.

"There you really are wrong, Mr. de Freyne. The boy was taken there as a treat."

"A *treat*! For whom? For him? What a strange idea—I mean, to think it could be a treat to go anywhere with her, Mrs. Wyburn."

"It is, rather," she acknowledged.

"Well, then, if that is really all that was troubling you, I do hope you're happy now?"

He said this with one of his subtle, insinuating changes of tone that were always so effective. Musicians will understand when I say it was like a change from the common chord in the minor to the dominant in the major. It was partly from force of habit, partly because he really wished to win Mrs. Wyburn over.

"Of course, now you've given the explanation it's, *so far*, all right. You'll have a cup of tea with me, won't you?"

"I should enjoy it particularly. Let me ring." After a minute or two she said—

"But perhaps I might venture to suggest it might be better—more prudent—if you were to go about a little less with Valentia? . . . Of course, I quite see now that you're so devoted to Romer, and like a brother and so forth, but I can't help considering what people say."

"Don't call Lady Totness people, Mrs. Wyburn! Think what a disagreeable, insincere woman she is—not a bit *femme du monde*, and so exceptionally stupid and spiteful!"

Harry stayed with her for an hour, having tea, chatting, telling her stories against every one she didn't like, and speaking with a kind of tender and admiring familiarity of both Valentia and Romer, in a way that at once reassured and flattered her.

Finally, she actually found herself begging Harry to use his influence with the young couple to be less frivolous and mondains, and not to be always going out, which he promised to do. She even confided to him her great wish that they had two or three children, which would steady them down, and he warmly agreed with her, but said that he felt that on that subject it was, perhaps, hardly for him to interfere.

Of course he confided in her, in his turn, how frightfully hard up one was, with no one buying pictures, and outsiders winning all the big races after having no earthly chance on any form they had shown that season. Mrs. Wyburn positively tried to talk racing with him for a minute or two—rather pathetically—but soon got out of her depth and fell back on Art. She said she thought, candidly, that Harry's portrait of his cousin was a pity.

They parted excellent friends, she even asking him as a favour not to tell Romer the reason of his visit. To Valentia he might mention it, as Mrs. Wyburn thought it might be a lesson to her.

Harry professed, at first, some little scruple on the point. He scarcely liked, he said, the idea of concealing it from Romer. They always told each other everything. But Mrs. Wyburn was afraid of her son's anger—which she could not endure, unless *she* was in the right— and of appearing ridiculously meddling. Harry owned that her conduct *might* seem rather malicious and absurd. At last he consented, and it was agreed that neither of them should ever say anything about it to Romer at all.

It is scarcely necessary to say that Harry kept his promise of silence to the letter. Had he not done so the story would at least have had the interest of novelty, for Romer had never yet heard anything about the expedition to the British Museum, and he never did.

A week or two later, when Mrs. Newhaven's ball at the Grafton Galleries was described in the paper, Mrs. Wyburn, who read the account, observed that there was no reference whatever to quadrilles of various nationalities—Egyptian or otherwise; and she rather wondered at the omission. But it did not occur to her to suppose that this portion of the entertainment had been entirely imaginary—a lurid figment of Harry's vivid fancy and fertile invention.

He left, it must be said, on the old lady a lasting impression—by no means an unfavourable one. Even when she had reason to grow seriously anxious again on the same subject, she never could bring herself in her own mind to blame Harry—she could not at heart think ill of him. She was only extremely angry with Romer and Valentia.

XI

THE FRIENDS

Harry had baffled Mrs. Wyburn for the time. He always dealt with his difficulties one by one as they cropped up, not *en masse*, and invariably in a manner that relieved the tension for a short time only—he rarely did anything radical.

His financial position was, however, growing rather serious, and occasionally the thought of Miss Walmer flitted through his mind.

To marry Miss Walmer would be far the quickest and simplest way out of his difficulties, and she would really be very little trouble, as little trouble, perhaps, as any wife could be. Besides, Harry had, with reason, great confidence in his own powers of dealing with women—getting whatever it was that he wanted from them, and afterwards preventing their being a nuisance. But he did not much like the idea of this mercenary marriage, because he was not in the least tired of his romance with Valentia, and saw great difficulties in the way of keeping it up later on. He had worrying doubts as to her consenting to revive it afterwards if he married.

Her grey eyes and soft fair hair with its dense waves held a lasting fascination for him. It has been well said that for each individual there exists in some other being some detail which he or she could find only in this particular person. It might be the merest trifle. Harry knew what it was in Val that had a specially compelling charm to him—it was the way her hair grew on her forehead. And there was something childlike in her expression that made a peculiar appeal to him. The power her face had over him was undiminished—it had begun seriously when he painted her portrait, and had grown gradually since then. And she was the only woman he had ever met whose affection for him did not cool his own enthusiasm. On the contrary, it was one of the things which held him to her most.

In a sense he was even loyal to her. Harry was not one of those extravagant Don Juans who made conquests solely for the gratification of their vanity by adding to their collection. Essentially cool and calculating, he used his attractiveness only when he thought it would be of some genuine value to him, or some real satisfaction. As a Lovelace he was economical.

Though a great connoisseur of feminine charm and beauty, and superficially susceptible and excitable, with all this, as many women knew, Harry was as hard as nails.

Valentia was the only woman for whom he had ever felt, besides the physical attraction, a kind of indulgent tenderness. This was partly, no doubt, because they had been fond of each other as children, and because of a racial sympathy, a *sentiment de famille* due to their relationship. But it was not really to be depended on.

No one could be a more charmingly devoted lover than Harry. There was no one like him for little attentions and inattentions, charming little thoughts, caressing words, and the little jealous scenes that women value. It was not the mere mechanically experienced love-making that women see through and to which they often prefer a clumsy sincerity. It was natural, spontaneous. He had, in fact, a genius for love-making, but he had not, like Romer, a genius for love. Harry had all the gift of expression—poor Romer had only the gift of feeling.

But notwithstanding Harry's magnetism, a woman once disillusioned by him was disillusioned for ever. Women never forgave him. His romances generally ended suddenly, and always irrevocably.

HARRY HAD NO GREAT LOVE of truth in the abstract, but, at least, he never deceived himself. He saw through his own unscrupulousness, and rather despised it just as he despised his own work as a painter. He had grown really fond of Van Buren for the simple, sincere qualities in which Harry knew himself to be deficient; and the American's whole-hearted admiration—almost infatuation—for him gave Harry the pleasure one feels in the frank devotion of a child. It touched him, even while he intended to make use of it, because it was his nature to make use of everything. It is an infallible sign of the second-rate in nature and intellect to make use of everything and every one. The genius is incapable of making use of people. It is for the second-rate clever people to make use of him.

One morning Harry had heard unexpectedly that he had sold a picture—a thing that rarely happened—and was looking at the cheque he had received, when Van Buren came into the studio. Harry told the news.

"Well, Harry, I do congratulate you, with all my heart! What are you going to do with that?"

"Frame it," said Harry. "It's the only one I've had for three years. It's a curiosity."

The American laughed.

"Harry, I guess what you're really going to do—you're going to give yourself the humble joy of paying some of the more pressing liabilities. I know you!"

"My dear fellow, that would be mad extravagance! Oh no. You see, this cheque is—just enough to be no earthly use."

Van Buren sat down.

"Harry, if you'd only let me. . . But I know that vexes you, so I won't talk of it. You're Quixotic, that's what's the matter with you." He smiled, pleased with the word. "Yes, Quixotic! I want to speak to you about your cousin—I mean Miss Daphne, the beauteous broo-nette."

"Well, how do you think you're getting on?" asked Harry, who already knew from Valentia that it was hopeless.

"Not as well as I should like, Harry. I can't say I feel I'm making any very great progress. She's a dream, but I'm afraid she regards me as a heavy-weight. She's only a child, really, I know. She would prefer a little boy of her own age who would make her laugh. Maybe she thinks I'm too old. What do you say?"

"You must give her time."

"I pay her every little attention that I can," said Van Buren seriously.

"Perhaps you're too attentive."

"I'd give her anything in the world she wanted, Harry, if she'd let me."

"Well, give her a miss for safety."

"What's that?"

"Why—this evening you're going to meet her at a dance, aren't you—at the Walmers'?"

"Yes; I'm looking forward to that."

"Well, don't go—don't turn up. Then she'll miss you. Say, tomorrow, you were prevented."

Van Buren began to smile.

"I see what you mean. It's an idea. You do hand me some good advice! Is it what you would do yourself, Harry?"

"It's what I'm always doing."

"But then I don't like the idea of being rude. One always wants to give the impression of being well-bred, no matter what the facts maybe."

"It won't be rude. She'll be thinking about you much more than if you were there, wondering why you're not."

"You mean it will keep her guessing, Harry?"

"That's the idea. I shan't say you're not coming. I'll pretend to be expecting you too."

"Well, perhaps I'll try that. I know I've only got an outside chance. She counts me as one of the also-rans."

"Are you really very devoted, old chap? Would you break your heart if it didn't come off?"

Van Buren thought a moment, then said with his scrupulous truthfulness—

"Well, no: I can hardly say that, Harry. I'm not so far gone as all that. But I think she's a very beautiful, charming, well-brought-up young lady—a typical English girl—a June rose, a real peach. She's the ideal of the sort of girl I'd like to marry. But if she's out of my reach—well, I should resign myself."

"Would you try for some one else? There are probably about a million girls just like that, you know, who would be only too delighted."

Van Buren shook his head.

"She's the only girl I should care about marrying. If it doesn't come off I shall go back to New York. And I do wish you'd come with me. A fellow with your talents would do splendidly there. Why, I'd find you a place in the Bank in New York. I'd see you made your fortune pretty quick. But you'd never leave London."

"I'm not so sure. Anyway, we'll give it a chance till the autumn."

"Yes, I must see it to a finish."

"If you don't settle down here, then, would you marry an American girl?"

"No. In that case I shan't marry at all. I shall settle down to the life of a lonely bachelor—choose the broad and easy path that leads to single misery, Harry." He laughed.

"Instead of the straight and narrow road that leads to married unhappiness," said Harry. "So you *are* very keen on Daphne?"

"Not exactly that, perhaps. But it must be her or no one for a life-partner. She's the only girl who ever made any appeal to me from the point of view of domestic life. When I think of a happy home and a fireside with her, it makes me curl like an autumn leaf."

"What a curious chap you are," said Harry, smiling.

"See here," said Van Buren, taking a letter out of his pocket. "I've got a letter from a lady—it's signed Flora Luscombe—but I don't seem to remember anything about her."

Harry took the letter. It was written on mauve paper in a somewhat straggling hand, and was dated from "Dimsdale Mansions, St. Stephen's Road, North Kensington." It was a pathetic, yet cheery invitation to tea.

"It's Miss Luscombe, of the Tank, as we call it," said Harry.

"Oh, the actress? Well, I think I shall go, Harry. I've never had the opportunity of mixing much in dramatic circles. It's real kind of her to have asked me, I must say. I didn't even remember her."

"No one ever remembers her. But it's amusing and absurd. You'll meet some of the people you like. Flora will show you round—point out all the obscurities there, and so forth. Oh, she's a good soul—old Flora."

"Is she old, Harry?"

"About twenty-three, or thirty-three. I like her, though she's rather a snob."

"Ah, they say all Americans are snobs, Harry, but I feel sure I'm not. Still, if I really liked a man I can't say I should turn against him even if he had a title."

"And if I really hated a person I should never get to like him, even if he had a bad reputation."

Van Buren looked surprised and impressed, also delighted.

"Is that a paradox, or an epigram, Harry?"

"I can't think!"

"Won't you tell me what it is?"

"It's bosh," said Harry impressively, "mere bosh!"

"Tell me what you really mean by it."

"How should I know? I haven't the very slightest idea," Harry said, stretching himself.

Van Buren looked thoughtfully out of the window.

"How do you suppose our ro-mances will end?"

"As badly as possible; romances always do," said Harry. "We ought to be only too thankful that they end at all."

"Why, I'm afraid you're a pessimist! How do you define a pessimist, Harry?"

"What a mania you have for definition, old chap! I think I agree with the little girl who said that an optimist is the man who looks after your eyes, and the pessimist the person who looks after your feet."

"Why, that's very subtle. I quite see what she means. There's a lot in that idea, Harry." He thought gravely.

"Is there? Well, come out to lunch."

XII

A Home Chat

Yes, Romer, on the whole I don't think our season's been a success. With any amount of struggle, worry, bother, clothes, motoring, and making up parties, we've just succeeded in not getting Daphne married to Van Buren, and putting your mother in a perpetual, constant, lasting bad temper."

"Have we?" said Romer.

He was sitting in an arm-chair listening, as usual, while Valentia talked. He did not always understand what she was saying, nor did he even always know the subject she was discussing, but he loved to hear her voice, that was like an incantation in his ears. He said a few words occasionally, desiring that the musical sound should continue.

"All our old friends seem to have grown dull and sensible except Harry, and he's been rather jerky and unsatisfactory—and all the new ones have turned out complete failures. When I say they're complete failures, of course I mean they've bored me. But, of course, it may not have been their object in life to do anything else."

"Yes."

"Look at Mr. Rathbone—a man like that, tattooed, and collecting old programmes of theatres. Well, he's as dull as ditchwater, perfectly stupid and always saying the right thing to the wrong people. Then Captain Foster, who seemed perfectly harmless and only decorative, turns out to be really dangerous, and to count. He's in love with Daphne, and he has got his mother, who is very weak and foolish and sentimental, round on his side, and Daphne's always going to tea or to lunch there, and they've utterly spoilt her—at least, her taste in hats has gone all wrong, and she told me that Mrs. Foster had pink paper shavings in her drawing-room fireplace, and asked me why I didn't have them too!"

"Really?"

"Yes. And though she's very good, I know it'll end in our having to give in, and a pretty wedding, and a tiny flat, and utter wretchedness! And Daphne will get to like old Mrs. Foster better than me, and they'll have five hundred a year at the most; and even if they aren't really miserable she'll have to gradually grow suburban, and come up to the theatre and have to rush off so as to catch the last train back to Boshan or Doddington or somewhere! I mean if they take a little house out of town—near Mrs. Foster. However, I'm not going to give in just yet. . . I could understand a slight sacrifice—or even a big one if I were in love with Captain Foster, but I'm not. I suppose you'll say that I needn't be, but that isn't the point. The utter absurdity is that all Daphne wants of him she could see now. No one minds her seeing him. But why should she break up her life and spoil her future for it? Of course, *that* part is *his* idea. He is so selfish that he isn't satisfied with the harmless fun they have now, but wants her to live all her life in a sort of workman's cottage or tenement building just for the sake of the joy, privilege, and honour of having every meal with him!"

"What a brute!" said Romer mildly.

"Isn't he? And suppose a war broke out, and that darling, handsome boy perhaps put an end to suddenly by a bullet, or mentioned in despatches, or something, and promoted—oh, please don't talk to me about it any more, Romer. I hate the life. But I suppose she'll have to go her own way."

Valentia paused and looked pensively in the glass.

"And dear Van Buren, he's been pretty badly treated, I think. I suppose he knows it isn't my fault or Harry's. I try to make up for it in lots of ways—by getting him an introduction to the man who wants to fly across the Atlantic. I really hoped he would say to Van Buren, 'Fly with me!' but he didn't, and in the most roundabout way and by the most fearful lot of trouble—chiefly through me—he was asked to dinner to meet that other man—I forget his name, the one who keeps on discovering the North Pole. And it seems he is a dear, and awfully good-looking. And then he—Van, I mean—has met Bernard Shaw, and Graham White, and Lloyd George, and Thomas Hardy, and Sargent, and Lord Roberts, and Henry James, and even Gabrielle Ray, so he hasn't had such a bad time in London. I don't see that he has anything to complain of, do you, Romer?"

"Shouldn't think so."

"That was what he wanted, you know," continued Valentia. "But if we couldn't get him a wife as well, it's not our fault. I'm sure we've tried our best. He's such a dear, and very fond of England. He has been most useful to Harry, I'm sure; and—I think the new fashions are simply frightful. The new way they're going to do the hair will be revoltingly unbecoming, and the whole thing will make every one look hopelessly dowdy. The smarter you are, the more of a frump you will look!"

"Oh, I say, Val!"

"Yes, you will—I mean I will, but I won't. . . Because I'm not going to follow the fashion like a sheep. And if you're not very careful I shall dress in a style of my own."

"Like a sheep! Do sheep follow the fashion?"

"Of course they do. Didn't you know that? What one does all the rest do. Of course it doesn't change so often—even in the best Southdown circles—at least *we* don't notice the change. When a new kind of 'baa' comes in and they all echo it we don't see any difference, but I don't suppose they see any difference in our fashions either. Oh, and Romer, I've been worried because I feel I've got so frightfully empty-headed and unintellectual through just *living*, never reading or thinking, when we go down to the Green Gate I shall read a lot of serious books. I'm going to read H. G. Wells, and Hichens, and Aristotle, and some history, and all sorts of 'improving' things. When are we going?"

"As soon as possible," said Romer, brightening up. "Let's go next Wednesday."

"Oh, I can't be ready quite as soon as that, Romer dear! Let's go on Tuesday. I'll arrange it all."

"Good!" said Romer, beaming.

"And I'll get Harry to come down with us."

"Thought he was going yachting with the Walmers?"

"Oh no, he's not, after all. . . He doesn't really care for the sea."

"Oh!"

"Harry, of course, is sorry for Van Buren," continued Valentia. "And yet he takes Daphne's part about Cyril Foster. He knows it's spoiling her, but he thinks she ought to be spoilt; he's so fond of Daphne."

"Why doesn't he marry her himself?" asked Romer.

"Harry?" She looked at him in surprise. "Why, Romer, what a harpist you are. If I've told you once, I've told you a hundred times, he never marries! Harry has a great many bad habits, goodness knows. But marrying isn't one of them."

"Do you think he's keen on some one else?" asked Romer after a rather long pause.

She seemed annoyed at the question, then smiled again.

"I don't know! The other day I called at the studio unexpectedly to ask for something I'd forgotten, and found Harry improvising at the piano—you know that way he has of improvising from memory—an inaccurate memory—of some well-known composer. I've never known him do it except when he wanted to—please some woman. Well, Lady Walmer was there, leaning over the piano and listening. Should you think from that he's keen, as you call it, on her?"

"Lady Walmer! At her age!"

"Why, Romer, she's no older than anybody else! It doesn't matter nowadays in the very slightest degree whether one is twenty-eight, or thirty-eight, or even forty-eight. To a modern man it's all exactly the same. Of course, if a flapper is what is required, well then, naturally, he must be shown to another department. But apart from that—why, Lady Walmer would be quite as dangerous a rival for me as a woman ten years or twenty years younger. And I'm not twenty-five yet."

"Rival to *you*? What do you mean?"

Romer stared at her, a spark of his fanatic admiration showing in his eyes.

She laughed and hurried on.

"Nothing. I never mean anything. I know what you think, Harry is not a marrying man, but he might become one. But a girl like Alec Walmer! With the figure of a suffragette and the mind of a canary who plays cricket, or a goose who goes in for golf—"

"Heaps of cash."

"Yes, I know. But Harry's an artist—he needs sympathy."

"He's got his head screwed on the right way."

"But his heart's in the right place."

"What is the right place?"

"Don't be irritating, Romer. We'll go to the Green Gate on Monday then. And now I must go out and order a short tweed skirt, and a garden roller, and a few other things that we shall need in the country. Leave it all to me! No, I never forget anything; even your mother says I'm practical. And oh, do let's try and put her in a good temper before we go away. You'd better go and see her and say good-bye today, early in the afternoon, alone. And then I'll go in late and take away the impression of anything you've said wrong. Do you see, darling? Dear Romer!"

She went out of the room like a sunbeam in a hurry.

Romer followed her with a wondering expression. To him her movements, her hair, her eyes seemed to suggest some fascinating language he had not yet learnt. She seemed to him almost a magic creature.

As usual, he showed his sensations simply by obeying. He went to say good-bye to his mother.

XIII

Valentia's Visit

Romer's mother, looking intensely cross—it was her form of deep thought—was re-embroidering, with extra little stitches, and unnecessary little French knots, and elaborate little buttonholes that would never see a button, a large and fine piece of embroidery on which she had been working for many months. She had that decadent love of minute finish in the unessential so often seen in persons of a nervous yet persistent temperament.

She was expecting her daughter-in-law. Romer had said, "Val will look in this afternoon."

Valentia arrived, delightfully dressed, and, to the casual observer, looking just as usual, but in her costume there was just that nuance of difference—what was it?—extra sobriety, a more subdued look—some trifle that she had worn last year to suggest to the seeing eye a hint of praiseworthy economy?—at any rate, a shade that other young married women would recognise at once as the right note when calling on one's mother-in-law.

Mrs. Wyburn greeted her with real pleasure, and with far more warmth than she ever showed to her son (her affection for him being authentic). The sight of Valentia, however, always genuinely raised her spirits. She was fascinated by her, and had an obscure desire to gain Valentia's liking, and even admiration—by force, if necessary! At the same time she felt jealousy, disapproval, an odd pride in the girl's charming appearance, and a venomous desire to give her slight pain.

"Romer has been here, I see—I mean, I guess he has by the cigarette. He's the only person who's allowed to smoke here. Yes, Mrs. Wyburn, we're off on Wednesday. Won't you miss us awfully? But I shall be very glad to go. I've really had enough of the season." Val spoke with a shade of weariness.

"No wonder! I suppose you've hardly had one quiet evening at home the last three weeks?"

"Very likely not one. Even when we're quite alone Harry comes round, and often his American friend too."

This was a challenge.

Valentia was sitting opposite the light, dressed in blue, in a black hat of moderate size, looking straight at the elder lady with a smile, and stirring her cup of tea.

Mrs. Wyburn admired her pluck and the fit of her dress.

"Yes, exactly—just what I should have thought. You know what a horror I have of displaying anything in the shape or form of *interference*, dear Valentia. But, since you've mentioned it yourself, may I just say, doesn't it seem almost a pity that you should never be alone with your husband?"

Valentia began to laugh.

"Oh, really, Mrs. Wyburn, why do you assume that? But of course we're longing for a quiet time. That is why we're going away so early. What *delicious* China tea! Yours is the only house where one gets it quite like this."

She put down her cup, which was more than half full, with a slight sigh.

"Romer hates China tea too," said Mrs. Wyburn. "It would be really better for your nerves if you'd drink it, my dear."

"And when do you go to Bournemouth?"

"The first week in August. So I shall be able to come down one day— as Romer asked me—before I go, and just have a peep at what you're all doing at the Green Gate."

She smiled with grotesque playfulness.

"Oh, that will be nice," said Valentia. "It must be looking lovely now. Did Romer say anything else of any importance?"

"He never says much, as you know, important or not! He's very like his poor father, who really used to sit opposite to me for hours at a time without opening his lips."

"A strong, silent man," murmured Val sympathetically. "I know so well what you mean."

"Indeed you don't," snapped Mrs. Wyburn. "He was the weakest creature—*morally*, I mean, poor dear—that ever breathed. He was a very tall, fine man, but yet any pretty woman could turn him round her little finger! It was his most marked characteristic."

"Fancy! Devoted to you, of course. Romer's often told me."

"I'm sure he hasn't. What can Romer know of my domestic troubles, as he was just four when he lost his poor father? But however that may be, I do hope, Valentia, you will wear warm, *sensible* clothes for the garden. I never quite like the idea of your sitting out on that little terrace late in the evening with practically nothing on your shoulders. People should be so careful of the night air."

"How thoughtful of you, Mrs. Wyburn! But I have a wrap—I never sit out without a wrap."

"Pink chiffon, I suppose?"

"Now how did you know? You seem to have second sight!"

"Yes; I guessed as much. Very candidly, dear Valentia, I don't approve of pink chiffon. But we women of an elder generation are never listened to, though our advice is worth hearing, I can tell you."

"Oh no, Mrs. Wyburn, don't say that. What would you advise instead then—a red crochet woollen shawl? I'll get one, of course. How lovely that embroidery is getting that you're doing! I remember last February thinking that it was as beautiful as it could be, and now it is more wonderful still. Let me look."

She bent down her pretty head to admire it.

"Is it my fancy, or the light, or hasn't your hair grown a little brighter in colour lately, Valentia dear?"

"Oh, do you really think so? I'm so glad. I was afraid it was just the same—just as it was in Harry's portrait of me, you know."

"It does look very like the portrait. But, very frankly—you won't mind my saying so?—I think that if it were not quite so fair it would be an improvement."

"Oh, naughty Mrs. Wyburn! Fancy your wanting me to touch up my hair—make it dark at the roots, I suppose, as so many people seem to do! Oh! I wouldn't! What would Romer say? He likes it like this."

Before the elder lady had quite recovered from the blow, Valentia went on carelessly—

"Daphne sent her love to you. She mayn't have time to come and see you before we leave."

"Has she been going to any more fancy balls as Rosalind?" asked Mrs. Wyburn sarcastically.

"No, oh no. There haven't been any more."

"I heard a report—oh, only a report—that Mr. Van Buren is a great admirer of your sister's; indeed, it was even said that they were going to be engaged."

This was really a sore subject to Valentia. Her temper began to waver slightly. It had been a very pet scheme of hers, and only Daphne herself had defeated it by refusing the millionaire. But of course she knew better than to tell Mrs. Wyburn that.

"Oh yes, you heard that. I believe he does admire her very much. But I hope I'm not going to lose Daphne yet."

Something in her expression warned Mrs. Wyburn, who said affectionately—

"Well, there's plenty of time; she's *so* young. I don't believe in girls marrying till they're sensible women and know something of housekeeping, and are fitted to deal with their servants."

"I hope you haven't been having any more trouble with yours lately?"

"Indeed I have! I had just sent for the housemaid to give her notice because she never dusts the lustres properly, when she turned round and gave it—notice, I mean—to *me!*"

"What a blessing! It saved you the trouble."

"On the contrary, if you knew anything of domestics, Valentia, you would see that it put me in a most awkward position—most awkward; and now I shall have to live at Mrs. Hunt's!"

"To live at Mrs. Hunt's?" repeated Val, as if stupefied. "Why, you're not going to leave your charming house? And who is Mrs. Hunt?—an old friend of yours?"

"Don't you really know who Mrs. Hunt is, Valentia?" Mrs. Wyburn's voice trembled.

"No; I haven't the faintest idea."

"She's a Registry Off—Well, may you never know! Certainly I'm not going to leave my house. The idea of such a thing!"

"Oh, I'm *so* glad," said Val, getting up. "I'm afraid I must leave it, though. I have so many little things to do before I go. Now, Mrs. Wyburn, take great care of yourself, and I do *hope* you'll get a nice housemaid quite soon. That sort of thing is so worrying, isn't it?"

Mrs. Wyburn accompanied her to the door, and as usual stood on the landing with her, complaining of various troubles, and finally parted with caressing words and advice about going for country clothes to "a little dressmaker—quite near here—who runs up one's blouses and skirts."

"Does she? Fancy! She must be small! Good-bye!" . . .

. . . "What a woman!" murmured Val as she got into the carriage.

"What a wife for Romer!" exclaimed Mrs. Wyburn as the door shut.

XIV

A Suggestion

Miss Luscombe, humming a tune, was wandering round her drawing-room, arranging it. She always hummed a little tune when she was alone, if possible some quaint old French air. Not that she was really alone now; only her invisible mother was with her. To do her justice, Flora took as much trouble to impress this almost imperceptible audience as if she represented a large crowd.

"There!" she said. She dusted a little blue vase and put it further back. "Now you're nice and tidy. No, you go back there, you ugly thing!" pouting at a photograph, "you're not wanted today! Come out more in the light, Lady Charles! We want you to be seen. *That's* better!"

From the depths of an arm-chair, where she was hidden, Mrs. Luscombe, who was watching her with intense irritation, said sharply—

"Who do you expect today?"

"Oh! how you startled me, Mummy! I didn't know you were there. . . Isn't it funny, when you wear that dark red dress, *just* the colour of the armchair, one doesn't see you?"

She went on humming in the low, sweet voice, "*La violette double, double—la violette double-ra-ra.*"

"Pray stop that, Flora. My nerves won't bear it. Who did you say you expect?"

"Mr. Rathbone, darling, if you *must* know. Mr. John Ryland Rathbone, to be exact. You know he's one of the Catford Rathbones, don't you, Mummy?"

"What's a Catford Rathbone?"

"Dear mamma!" she laughed. "It's quite a good old family. One of the untitled aristocracy."

"I thought you told me his father was a farmer?"

"No, dear—that's a little mistake. I told you his father had *taken* to farming—as a hobby. Besides, that's just what I mean—a fine old yeoman stock—the backbone of the country."

"Why are you praising up this Mr. Backbone—or Rathbone—so much? Is he in love with you?"

Flora laughed coquettishly, putting on her Russian Princess manner. It was voluble, disdainful, and condescending. She often changed, quite suddenly, from an *ingénue* to a *grande dame*, and then to an adventuress and back again before you knew where you were.

"Of course he's in love with me. What of that? Poor boy, he must take his chance like the others! '*La violette double, double—*' Oh, I forgot, dear. I beg your pardon."

"What's he coming here for?" pursued the relentless mother.

Miss Luscombe now became a soubrette of a somewhat hooligan type, and pretended to throw a little feather duster she was holding into the depths of the arm-chair.

"That remains to be seen. But I'm a girl who knows how to take care of herself. I shall keep him in his place, old dear. Don't you worry."

"I don't."

There was a ring at the door. Flora blushed genuinely, and put some powder on. She became sweet and tactful again, and refined, the amiable woman of the world. She helped her mother out of the arm-chair, quite unnecessarily, but perhaps to hurry her departure.

"You'd better leave us alone now, darling," she said, "and girlie will tell you all about it afterwards."

Mrs. Luscombe ran like a hare through a side door.

The servant announced, throwing open the folding doors, "Mr. Rathbone."

In two seconds the feather-duster was behind a screen, and Flora, looking really very handsome—she was, as usual in the daytime, in semi-evening dress—was reading a little book covered in old vellum, and kept for the purpose of her being found reading it. She put it down and welcomed her guest charmingly.

Rathbone, looking very fair and pink and rather determined, had brought with him a kind of case containing his collection of old theatre programmes, so that he gave the impression of being a diplomat of high importance with a portfolio.

She helped him prettily to show her the programmes, and was pleased to see that there was something else on his mind.

She gave him a cigarette and they had tea. He told her the ancient story of his writing to Cissie Loftus, and how he had never received an answer. She welcomed the anecdote as though it combined the brilliance of a jewel with the freshness of a daisy.

Then he spoke in a somewhat thick voice and with that rather gruff manner that she associated with sincerity.

"Miss Luscombe, I. . ."—he sighed deeply. "To tell you the truth, there's something—for a long time I've wanted to ask you."

He fixed on her intently his blue eyes, in which there was an ardent glare.

"Really, Mr. Rathbone? What can I do for you?"

"A great deal. The question is, what would you do for me?"

"Oh, that depends," she said, smiling, looking down, and enjoying herself.

"Not to put too fine a point upon it, Miss Luscombe—;" he stopped nervously.

"Miss Luscombe sounds so formal," she murmured.

"You wouldn't allow me to call you Flora, would you?"

He smiled, but she thought he looked disappointed. Perhaps he was a man who needed difficulties—opposition.

"Well. . . I. . . it depends," she said.

"Look here, Flora, you're a very charming woman. I have a great admiration for you. What is more, I believe you to be a thoroughly good—" he hesitated again; was he going to say "woman," "actress?"—he decided on "sort."

"Oh!"

"Now I'll reveal to you the dream of my life, which I wouldn't tell to anybody else."

"I wonder if I can guess it?" she said, wishing he would hurry up. Lady Charles was coming at half-past five to get the address of that fur place Flora knew of, where you got things practically for nothing—and they were worth it, too.

"I know I'm not so very young," continued the young man.

"Why, you're only about thirty-four, aren't you? I call that young."

"Do you—do you really? Now I was afraid I was getting rather too old to begin, as it were, a fresh life. Well now"—he came a little nearer and touched her hand, which lay on the table; it was a pretty hand, thin and bony, with pink polished nails and a garnet ring—"will you do it for me? will you help me? will you not think me foolish—too daring—too sanguine? . . ."

"What?"

"Yes. I see you've guessed. Yes. I want to go on the stage."

XV

MISS WALMER

And so you see, don't you, Lady Walmer, that I really simply couldn't do it—I mean I must do it. They're expecting me there for the whole summer. How could I throw them over at the last minute?"

Harry spoke in his most convincing voice. He was calling on Lady Walmer, and they were both sitting in her little yellow boudoir. She had just come in from a bazaar, and was wearing a rather angry-looking hat, very much turned up on one side, with enormous purple feathers. She was looking very far from pleased. Her handsome chin appeared squarer than usual. There was a look in her eyes that more than one man besides Harry would have been by no means anxious to meet.

She drew off her gloves, stroked one over the other thoughtfully, and said—

"Why did you promise to come on the yacht? The whole summer's spoilt for Alec."

"I hoped I could—I thought I could manage it. Surely you understand—"

"But it's got to come to that sooner or later, Harry. You can't make an omelette without breaking eggs. If you want to be a respectable, dull married man, you'll have to dissolve your romance, you know. I should have thought you were the last person to be weak about anybody else's feelings!—No, it's your own, my dear boy."

Harry's colour rose a little.

"My dear Lady Walmer! I'm going to tell—my cousin Valentia—all about it—I mean about my hopes. I'm certain that she will be charming about it—only too glad, for my sake."

"Oh! And yet I thought she was human! Or—is there some one else?"

"Certainly there's some one else—there's Romer. She's very devoted to him."

"Harry, my boy, we should get on so very much better if you wouldn't tell so many unnecessary fibs," remarked the lady.

She stood up and drew the hatpins out of her hat.

He said, "I'm quite frank with you. I don't think I've been anything else. And, after all, I only ask to do it in my own way—at my own time. To choose my moment. Really, one can't behave like an *impossible bounder*."

"Oh, can't one? Well, perhaps not."

She took the hat off and put it on a table, giving the impression suddenly, without it, of being smooth, a little bald, and very good-tempered.

"Then you'll forgive me, Lady Walmer—you'll understand? I should think that in about three or four weeks I shall be able to join you somewhere. But, about fixing the date—that's impossible. Can't I see Alec today?"

She smiled graciously.

"Certainly you may; I want you to. You must cheer her up and say nice things to her. Poor child, I wish she weren't so ridiculously pleased with you. You don't care two straws for her."

"I give you my word of honour that I will make her happy."

"I suppose you'll make her as happy as any one would. It's always something to get one's wish, even if the wish is a failure."

"Now, why do you say that? It won't be a failure."

"All right. I'll send her to you. Now be a good boy, Harry. I'm jealous—for Alec—of the Green Gate." She smiled in her attractive way. "Will there be an absolute rupture between you and your. . . cousins, do you think?"

"Oh, good heavens, Lady Walmer, no!" said Harry rather irritably. "We shall all be perfect friends, of course. . . what impossible things you expect."

"I expect only what is certain."

She went away.

Vanity was as elemental in Harry as in any other good-looking young man. With him, though, it was not a mere useless pursuit—an art-for-art's-sake joy—but invariably calculated and used as a means to an end.

He looked in the glass earnestly, then started as Alec came in.

He was always surprised and even a little *gêné* each time he saw her, by her immense apparent height. It seemed so much greater than it was because of the somewhat monotonous lines of her figure and her rather bird-like face.

Harry watched her, listened to her as she chattered away her hurried, inexpressive unmeaning slang, and looked at him with her bright, small, beadlike eyes.

He did not appreciate her. He did not know that behind the jerky manner and inexpressive face there was a Soul.

She had not been trained to talk sentiment, and she could not express her ideas; so, though she adored Harry, she only said to her mother in confidence, when in a serious mood, that he was all right; and when in a more playful frame of mind to her girl-friends, that he was a little *bit* of all right.

"Alec," he said, making her sit down in the lowest chair (he could not bear her towering over him), "isn't it a bore that I can't come on the yacht?"

"Pretty useless," she answered.

He took her hand.

"You won't forget me while I'm away, will you, Alec?"

"What do *you* think?" she answered in a trembling voice, and then gave a loud laugh.

"I don't think—I don't know."

"Oh, shut up!"

"Will you be just as nice when I see you again?" continued Harry, in a carefully-modulated voice.

"Why do you ask me all this rot?" she said, with another uneasy laugh. "Of course I shall."

"Good."

Harry couldn't think of anything else to say. Then he remembered. . .

"When I join you again I'm going to bring you a ring. What's your favourite stone?"

"Rubies and diamonds," she answered without a moment's hesitation. "I say, how sporting of you! That'll be ripping!"

He tried to feel touched by her artless joy. He knew he was not an ideally ardent suitor.

"Well, we'll have a good time later on, eh?" he said in her own tone.

"Don't be a silly ass!" replied the girl, her eyes full of tears and tenderness, and her heart of the most sincere joy and affection.

Harry laughed.

"Tell me, Alec, is your mother a soothing companion? Is she a nice woman to live with?"

"Oh! *she's* all right. A bit off colour sometimes. At least—well, she *is* all right, if you understand—and yet she's *not*—if you know what I mean."

"Ah! that is a dark saying. You are pleased to be mysterious—sphinx-like."

"You *are* a rotter, Harry!"

"How subtle you are, Alec. How elusive is the lightning-play of your wit!"

"*How* much?"

"The random poppy of paradox grows too often in the golden cornfield of your conversation," Harry went on, taking her hand.

"Oh, rats!" exclaimed the artless girl. "Can't make out what you're driving at half the time, when you go on like that. Don't believe you know yourself."

"Don't I? Really now, you know, we're almost—well—privately engaged. May I kiss you, Alec?"

She blushed crimson, turned her face away, and said, "Please yourself."

Unable to help laughing, he kissed the top of her head, told her to write to him, and left the house, feeling like an entirely new and recently-discovered kind of bounder.

He hated the double game. It didn't amuse him a bit. But now he felt he was free for a month's holiday, during which he had, however, the unpleasant holiday task of breaking the news to Valentia.

He was driving home, but changed his mind and called out to the cabman to drive to Valentia's house.

He found her trying on furs—furs in mid-summer!

She greeted the arrival of his exquisite discrimination and taste with clapped hands, soft, beaming eyes, and her smile—Valentia's smile. Miss Walmer couldn't smile at all—she didn't know how. She could only laugh.

XVI

Mrs. Foster

Daphne had come to say good-bye to Mrs. Foster.

This lady lived in a kind of model cottage in a garden in Ham Common. It was not at all like the ideal, 'quaint' model cottages that one sees advertised by well-known firms of furnishers, though it might have been. Mrs. Foster was rebellious to Waring, and sincerely disliked anything modern.

The little drawing-room, and indeed every other room in the house, was principally furnished by photographs and groups of her son Cyril— Cyril as a very plain boy, in a skirt, with hardly any eyes or hair, and a pout; Cyril as a 'perfect pet' of a sailor, at six. Then Cyril in cricketing groups (how he stood out against the other ordinary boys!)—in Etons (looking neat and supercilious), and then in his uniform, in which he looked simply lovely.

Daphne had an intense and growing desire to please his mother. In fact, curiously, she was more anxious to gain her approbation than that of Cyril himself. To this end she usually remade her hats, when possible, in the train on her way to Ham Common, and her pocket when she arrived there was usually filled with artificial flowers, feathers, or other ornaments that she had taken off her hat, so as to look simple. Also she turned it down all the way round to make it look as if it were merely a protection from the sun—not a hat.

Today she wore a pink-spotted muslin dress and a straw hat, with pink ribbon. She certainly looked extremely pretty, and not at all what she had such a dread of before Mrs. Foster, smart. Mrs. Foster had a horror of smartness in the *jeune fille*.

Daphne delighted her. She was a very sentimental woman, with a strong theoretical bias for the practical. She was by way of teaching Daphne housekeeping and how to manage on a small income (of which art she knew very little herself, but was supposed to know a great deal because she wore a kind of cap). She had a pretty, delicate, kind face, and was wearing large wash-leather gloves, in case she should wish to do a little gardening later on.

Daphne had still much of the child in her, and there was nothing she enjoyed quite so much as gardening with Mrs. Foster, and occasionally stopping to eat a gingerbread-nut, and hear something about Cyril and the brilliant remarks he had made as a child.

Mrs. Foster had a chiffonnier of a kind Daphne had never seen before, which fascinated her because such queer delightful things came out of it in the middle of the morning—slices of seed cake, apples, and the gingerbread-nuts. There were pink shavings in the fireplace, and wherever there was not a photograph of Cyril there was one of the Prince Imperial. Evidently he had been the passion of Mrs. Foster's earlier life. She loved to tell the story of how she had seen him at Chislehurst, and how she thought he had looked at her.

There were other nice things in the cottage: there were two rather large vases of pink china on which were reproduced photographs of Cyril's great-uncle and great-aunt—one in whiskers, the other in parted but raised hair with an Alexandra curl on the left shoulder. In these vases folded slips of paper called spills were kept. A modern note was struck by the presence of a baby Grand—a jolly, clumsy, disproportioned youthful piano, rather like a colt, on which Daphne played Chopin to Mrs. Foster, and sometimes The Chocolate Soldier to Cyril; and Mrs. Foster, at twilight, sometimes played and even sang, "*I cannot sing the old songs, they are too dear to me,*" which her mother used to sing, or, coming a little nearer to the present, "*Ask nothing more, nothing more, all I can give thee, I give,*" a passionate song of the early eighties.

No one, except Daphne, ever did ask any more.

The whole thing was, to Daphne, a treat. Something in the atmosphere of Ladysmith Cottage—that was its name—fascinated and amused her.

Mrs. Foster was a widow. Her husband had been a distinguished soldier. Almost the whole of her extremely small income had been devoted to Cyril's education, and with the assistance of an uncle who took interest in him, he had been got into the Guards, where he existed happily with a comparatively small allowance.

Mrs. Foster had not been at all surprised or annoyed at his wishing to marry at twenty-two. She thought it extremely natural. It seemed to her very sensible of Daphne to accept him, and that she was the most fortunate girl in existence.

"I hope your sister doesn't mind my taking you away from the gay, fashionable world for a day?" she archly asked.

"Oh no, of course not. We're going in the country next week, so I wanted to see you."

"Cyril's at Aldershot. I don't think he'll be able to come down this afternoon. He can't get away this week, I'm afraid."

"I shall see him before I go," said Daphne.

"Do you have a letter from him every day, darling?"

"Oh yes, a few lines."

"He is a noble boy!" said Mrs. Foster enthusiastically. "How he always hated writing letters! I remember how I guided his little hand to write his first letter to his uncle, General Rayner. Just as we got to the end of the letter Cyril suddenly jumped up and threw over the table. The letter was simply drenched in ink. Dear boy! I've got it still. . . Oh, you must come into the garden, Daphne. I've something new to show you. A friend of mine has just let her house. She didn't know what to do with her dovecot—nobody wanted it—so she's given it to me. Come and see the dear little creatures—they are so pretty."

They went out into the garden and stood looking at a sort of depressed pigeon-house.

Mrs. Foster made strange noises, which she thought suitable to attract the inmates, and Daphne saw two doves who struck her as if they had married in haste and were repenting at leisure.

"Why don't you let them go free?" suggested the girl. "Just think how happy and delighted they'd be."

"I doubt it. I don't think they'd know what to do with their freedom. They're not used to my garden yet, that's what's the matter. I do wish they would coo; perhaps they will a little later on." (This was a favourite expression of Mrs. Foster's.) "I want to see one perched on your shoulder, Daphne. It would make such a pretty picture."

"I'd rather give them something to eat," said Daphne.

Mrs. Foster started.

"Oh yes, of course. I fed them all yesterday afternoon, but I forgot about them this morning. Henry! Henry!"

The smallest boy appeared that had ever been called by that name.

"Henry, feed the doves."

"Yes, ma'am."

"Then bring the watering-can. We're going to water the flowers."

Henry, who seemed of a morose nature, went to obey.

"I'm obliged to have a boy for the knives, and he acts as a gardener when I'm busy," explained Mrs. Foster. "There isn't much of a kitchen garden, only a few gooseberries and apples, as you know, dear, but it's nice to think they grow there, isn't it?"

"Very."

"Of course, I can't make much show with them. Henry always eats them before they're ripe, which is *rather* hard. But he's a good, honest boy. One of his sisters has gone in for making blouses—in the village, you know. She's a brave girl, and I feel sure will get on."

"She must be! Have you ever. . . ?"

"Oh *no*. Of course not. *I* couldn't. When a woman reaches a certain age, my dear, a certain style is necessary. I don't mean great expense, but simple little things that would suit you, darling, wouldn't do for me. Now that little pink thing that you're wearing—I should look *nothing* in it, and yet I dare say Henry's sister. . . Where did you get it, dear?"

"Well, it *came* from Paquin's," said Daphne. "It's not new."

"Oh! Well, we mustn't be always talking of chiffons together, that's very frivolous. You're fond of poetry, aren't you?"

"Not so very," said Daphne truthfully.

"But you would like to hear mine; I know you would, dear," said Mrs. Foster, nodding, and patting her hand. "Dear girl, you shall. I've got a tiny little volume, all in manuscript. It's quite a secret, darling. Hardly any one—now—knows that I was poetical. But I can tell you anything—you're so sympathetic. I had at one time a great wish to be a sort of—not exactly Elizabeth Barrett Browning, or Christina Rossetti—you know who I mean, don't you?"

"Oh yes."

"But a singer of songs—songs of feeling. Well, let us go into the garden. I will show it to you later."

They sprinkled a few dead flowers, picked a few weeds, and then Mrs. Foster became thoughtful, took off her gloves, and went to her room and remained there for some time. She came down with a manuscript book in her hand. It had a shiny cover, and in the right-hand corner a piece of the cover was cut out. On the paper, showing through, was written in Mrs. Foster's delicate handwriting, "Fireflies of Fancy."

"This," she said, patting it, "is my little book, and after lunch I'll read you some of the poems, dear Daphne, though I'm not at all sure that all of them are quite suitable for you to hear."

"Oh, Mrs. Foster!" Daphne found difficulty in believing it.

"You see," continued the delicate-looking old lady, in her sweet, refined voice, "I was very much under the influence of the Passionate

School—Swinburne, Rossetti, Ella Wheeler Wilcox, and so on—at the time that I wrote. My husband never wished me to publish them. He didn't like them—he didn't understand them. I don't mind admitting to you, dear, that since I lost him I have sent one or two of the less—well—shall we say strongly coloured?—poems to the magazines at times, of course under a *nom de plume*. But they were all returned. I think they were considered too—well, too—However, I've given up the idea of making a name as a poetess now, and very rarely show them to anybody; *very* rarely."

Daphne answered, with absolute sincerity, that she was dying to see them.

After lunch, when they retired to the little drawing-room, Mrs. Foster sat down with her back to the light, and a slight flush on her cheek, and took up the book.

Daphne sat in a low little crimson arm-chair exactly opposite her, clasping her knees, her brown eyes fixed with the greatest interest as Mrs. Foster turned and turned the pages as if unable to select a suitable verse.

Then she began to read, in her soft, yet rather high voice, which seemed suited only to gentle greetings and adieux, or quavering orders to Henry.

"Night Time

He glanced as he passed,
And I hope, and I quiver,
I howl and I shudder with pains;
And like a she-tiger
Or overcharged river,
My blood rushes on through my veins."

She stopped suddenly.

"No, no, dear. I won't read this. Wait a minute. I remember now that was the one that was returned because it was too—er—I'll find you another one."

"Oh, do finish that one," said Daphne, "please! Isn't the light too much for your eyes?"

She jumped up quickly and pulled down the blind an inch or two, and then came back, having controlled herself.

Mrs. Foster looked at her rather sharply, and took no notice of what she supposed was emotion.

"Ah, here is something more suited to you, darling."

Spring

A Question, and an Answer

Will all the year be summer-time,
And each night have a moon?
Ah no, the Spring will quickly go,
And winter cometh soon.

And will your clasp warm mine like wine?
And will you love me true?
Ah no, the autumn leaves arrive,
And we must bid adieu.

"That's a rather pretty thing, in its way, isn't it?" she said.
"Very."
"Here's one more.

A Remembrance

Seems it well to see
A wild honey bee
Gold in the sun,
Ere day is done,
Sitting on a rose,
As the summer time grows.

Ah, the bold, brave days,
Ere the glass of Time
'Neath the sun's rays,
Like a flame of fire,—
And the . . ."

She stopped again.
"No, I don't think this is quite—"
"Do, do go on!"

Mrs. Foster looked at her.

"You have a great deal of sensibility, Daphne. I believe you have tears in your eyes."

"No, I haven't really." She turned away her head, nearly choking.

A loud knock was heard at the front door.

Mrs. Foster looked out of the window.

"It's Cyril!" she exclaimed. "He's got away after all. Quick! Quick!" She threw the book under a cushion and sat on it. With trembling fingers she took up some needlework out of a basket.

"Not a word—not a word! Go and meet him in the hall, dear. He's come to give us a surprise. I'll wait."

Blushing and laughing Daphne ran downstairs.

XVII

Engaged

Daphne and Cyril sat in the garden together. The conditions seemed ideal. It was a lovely afternoon; the sun was hot, but a gay irresponsible little west wind stirred the trees; bees hummed industriously, butterflies darted casually about among the few flowers, and even the reticent doves cooed from time to time, condescendingly. Peeping through the blind Mrs. Foster thought the two young people made a perfect picture, and was reminded of the Golden Age. Indeed, they had very much the charming, almost improbable air of the figures in a Summer Number of an illustrated paper. Perhaps the conditions were too perfect: the lovers had, of course, nothing to sit on but a rustic seat—Mrs. Foster would have thought it a crime to have anything else in a garden, and rustic seats are, no doubt, picturesque, but they are very uncomfortable; they seem to consist of nothing but points and knobs, gnarls and corners.

When Daphne was alone with Cyril like this she felt contented and peaceful at first, and then she began to wonder why she wasn't happier still—why she didn't feel ecstatic. She was proud of Cyril; he looked very handsome in flannels, his regular features, smooth fair hair, small head and small feet all added to his resemblance to the hero in the holiday number.

Cyril said—

"Dear little girl!" and took her hand.

She laughed and answered—

"Dear old boy!"

Then he said—

"By Jove! you do look ripping, Daphne."

She smiled.

"Jolly being here like this, isn't it?" said Cyril.

"Isn't it?" she answered.

"Jolly day, too."

"Yes."

"Wasn't it lucky I was able to get away?"

"Rather."

"It was a fearful rush."

"It must have been."

"Jove, it is hot!"

There was a pause.

"Darling!"

"Dear boy!"

"May I smoke a cigarette, dear?"

"Yes, do."

He lit a cigarette, and then put his arm round her waist.

"Don't, Cyril."

"Why not?" he asked, removing it.

"Oh, I don't know. Henry or some one might see."

"What's Henry?"

"A sort of gardener boy—the boy whose sort of sister makes kind of blouses in the village."

"Oh, does he matter?"

Cyril was wondering if he could ask for a drink.

When they were left entirely alone, on purpose to be free, he always felt rather shy and awkward, and intensely thirsty.

Daphne began to think about what time it was, and about her train back—subjects that never occurred to her when she was alone with Mrs. Foster.

"I'm afraid I shall soon have to be going," she said.

"Oh, I say! What, the moment I've arrived?"

He tried not to feel a little relieved. He wondered why he hadn't more to say to her. He had been desperate to get consent to their engagement, and was always extremely anxious and counting the minutes till they met, and when they were together, alone after much elaborate scheming, he felt a little embarrassed, and, like his fiancée, was surprised he wasn't happier.

"I say, Daphne!"

"Yes, dear."

"You do look sweet."

"Do you really think so?"

"Simply ripping! I say!"

"Yes."

"Won't it be jolly when we're married?"

"Yes; lovely."

"It will be all the time just like this, you see—only nicer. . . I say! Isn't it hot?"

They sat holding hands, he looking at her admiringly, she feeling mildly pleased that such a dear, handsome boy should be so fond of her. In the minds of both was another sensation, which they did not recognise, or, at all events, would not admit to themselves. They both, especially Cyril, counted the minutes to these *tête-à-têtes*, and immediately afterwards looked back on them with regret, feeling they had missed something. They wrote to each other frequent, short, but intensely affectionate letters about the happiness these interviews had given them. Yet, while they actually lasted, both Cyril and Daphne, had they only known it, were really rather bored. The next day, or the same evening, Cyril would write to her:—

"My own Darling,—How jolly it was having you a little to myself today! And to think that you really care for me!" and so on.

And she would enjoy writing back:—

"Dearest,—Didn't we have a heavenly time in the garden yesterday?" and so forth.

AS A MATTER OF FACT, they had not had a heavenly time at all; when he kissed her, which he sometimes did, she did not really like it, though she knew she ought, and it gave her a sort of mental gratification to think that he *had* given this manifestation of love, as she knew it was considered the right thing.

He did not really regard her as a woman at all, but more as a lovely doll, or sweet companion, and it pleased his vanity immensely to think he should be allowed this privilege, which at the same time seemed to him a little unnecessary, and even derogatory to her, though he enjoyed it very much too, in a somewhat uncomfortable way.

The fact that their engagement was so indefinite, that they had hardly any hope of being married for at least two years, perhaps added a little to the *gêne* of these meetings. The instant they were separated he began to long to see her alone again. Daphne felt sure she must be really in love because she took comparatively little interest in anything that was not more or less connected with the idea of Cyril. Perhaps she enjoyed the things she associated with him more than his actual presence. Talking about him to Valentia, or hearing about him from his mother, seemed more amusing and exciting than sitting with him alone and holding his hand. She would have liked best never to see him except in evening dress at a party, only to hear about him or think about him all day.

Cyril was sure that his feeling was real love, because he did not care two straws how hard up they should be when they were married, and because if he heard any one sing a sentimental song, however badly, he immediately thought of her with the greatest tenderness. He believed he missed her every moment of the day, and he took great trouble to see her, especially when there was a chance of their being alone. But, as a matter of fact, he was rather glad when Mrs. Foster came out into the garden; and when he had seen Daphne off at the station, although it was a pang to see her go away without him, it was perhaps also a slight relief.

When Val came to meet her at the station, full of news about the extraordinary number of exciting things that had happened in the day, and they dashed back to dress for a dinner Harry was giving before going to a dance, Daphne felt a tinge of sentiment and regret for the idyllic happiness in the garden, and began to count the hours until they should meet alone again. The glamour always returned an hour or so after they had been separated.

XVIII

AT THE CARLTON

With characteristic amiability, combined with that courage which had caused impatient people, who snubbed her in vain, to say she had the hide of a rhinoceros, Miss Luscombe had accepted the blow of Rathbone's proposal—the proposal which she had taken for an offer of marriage, but which was really an offer to go on the stage. She set to work at once making little efforts (most of which she knew to be futile) to arrange the matter. After all, if she should succeed in getting him some sort of a part, mightn't he, out of gratitude? . . . And she saw visions. Again, he had evidently got it very badly, this mania for acting and dressing up, and he had really quite enough money, if he chose to devote it to this object only; why shouldn't he take a theatre—make himself the manager and *jeune premier*, or, for the matter of that, *vieux dernier*—it really didn't matter—and let her be the leading lady? That was if he failed in every other scheme. She wrote letters to various people whom she knew on the stage, mentioning Rathbone's enormous willingness to take *anything*, his gentlemanly appearance, and, she felt sure, really *some* talent, though no experience. Most people took no notice, but after a while she received an offer for him to play one of the gentlemen in the chorus of *Our Miss Gibbs* in a second-rate little touring company of the smaller northern provincial towns.

It was an excuse for an interview, certainly; but this for a man who wished to play Romeo! And if, in his enthusiasm, he should actually accept it, it would take him away from her. However, hearing that she had some news for him, he, in his delighted gratitude, asked her to tea at the Carlton.

THEY WERE SEATED IN THE Palm Court eating their tea-cakes and sandwiches to the sound of "The Teddy Bear's Picnic," which made one feel cheerful and reckless, followed by "Simple Aveu," a thin, sentimental solo on the violin that made one feel resigned and melancholy. It was played by a man with a three-cornered face and a very bald head, who gazed at the ceiling as if in a kind of swoon—a swoon that might have been induced either by tender ecstasy or acute boredom.

All around them were noisy Americans, neatly dressed, and a good many prim, self-conscious ladies on the stage who had come on from their *matinées* and were accompanied mostly either by very young and rather chinless adorers, or by fat, fatuous men with dark moustaches, hair inclined to curl, and clothes a shade too gorgeous.

Here and there a simple, provincial-looking family were to be seen who had come up for a few days and had been to an afternoon performance, and were talking with great animation of the rights and wrongs of the hero and heroine of the play. It was characteristic of the provincials that they were really excited about the play itself, hardly knowing who were performing, while the suburbanites took interest only in the actors, all of whom they knew well by name and reputation, even their private life—at least, as much of it as got into the *Prattler*, *The Perfect Lady*, and *Home Chirps*.

On the whole it was a very characteristic London crowd, in that it consisted almost entirely of desirable aliens. Here and there, indeed, one saw a thin, slim, pretty woman with a happy but bothered-looking young man, both obviously English, who talked in low tones, and were evidently at some stage or other of a rose-coloured romance; but they were the exception.

Amidst this noisy and confused clientèle, with its showy clothes and obvious feminine charms, Miss Luscombe looked a strange, stray, untidy hothouse plant. She was odd and artificial, and dressed like nothing on earth, in pale and faded colours; but she was not vulgar. She was rather queer and delicate, and intensely amiable. Her self-consciousness made no claim on one; she was not exacting—always pleased and good-tempered. Rathbone recognised these qualities in her, and liked her better today, amidst the scent of the tea-cakes and cigarettes and the whine of the violin, than he had ever liked her before.

Pink, fair, calm, clean, and really hardly anything else, except extremely correct, and always good form, without being too noticeably so, no one would have dreamed that this quiet young man, who looked like a shy subaltern, was simply dying to disport himself on the stage, and that it was the dream of his life to make an utter ass of himself as Hamlet, or a hopeless fool of himself as (say) the hero in *Still Waters Run Deep*—a play he had seen as a boy and had always longed to act in.

She had broken the news to him.

"Miss Luscombe, do you mean to say that is the very best you can do for me?"

She explained the difficulties.

He was only one of so many! Unless the name was known it was frightfully difficult—even for geniuses—to get on. Of course, he might try, and go and see the various managers himself, but, frankly, probably nothing would come of it.

He was deeply depressed. What should she suggest?

"Might I ask if you care very, very much?" she asked.

"You might. I do." Yes. His heart was set on it.

Was it really? Well, if he simply hadn't the strength to go on living another day without going on the stage, the only thing, clearly, was just to hire a theatre and *go* on! A *matinée*, perhaps. Why not Romeo?

"And why not Juliet?" said he, rather rashly.

"Oh, that would be lovely!"

Her attention wandered at this moment. A very pretty, fair woman was rising from behind a palm where she had been seated with her back to the room. She went out rather quickly, followed by a good-looking young man with a single eye-glass.

"They have been trying to hide!" she exclaimed. "What a joke! It's that sweet Valentia Wyburn and Harry de Freyne. They must have been here when we arrived, for we should have seen them come in. I wonder what they came for?"

"To have tea, perhaps?" suggested Rathbone, after deep thought, shrewdly.

"Yes, yes, I know. But why hide like that?"

"Perhaps they didn't want to be seen," said Rathbone brilliantly.

"Yes, of course, but why not? I hope it doesn't show. . ."

"Well, it shows there's nothing in it, or they wouldn't come here."

"Does it?" said Miss Luscombe, rather disappointed.

"Well, where's the harm in being here? Ain't we here?"

"Oh yes, of course; but that's different. They're cousins, too, of course; I had forgotten."

"I don't see why you should worry if Romer doesn't," said Rathbone.

Before they left Rathbone had very nearly promised to see about engaging a theatre, and either for a charity or as an invitation *matinée*, rope, as he expressed it, all his friends in, lock the door, and force them to see him play Romeo to Miss Luscombe's Juliet.

Flora was deliriously happy at the idea, but had too much experience to rely on it, and was quite prepared to be thrown over for another more professional actress, and asked to play one of the ladies at the ball in the first act instead, probably in a mask. She went home and read over her one good notice—a great treasure—that had appeared in an evening paper, and had spoken of her as "*a young actress with a bright and winsome personality*." That was in a very small part, ten years ago. Would she ever get another real chance?

XIX

At Miss Westbury's

M rs. Wyburn found Miss Westbury being sensible and decided and holding forth about things in general to one or two friends over the tea-cups. Something in the way the old lady sat down and unfastened her mantle, so as to be sure to feel the benefit of it when she went out again, made the other women present feel that they were not wanted, and Miss Westbury did not attempt to detain them. For (though she would not have put it like that) she knew that she would get more fun out of her friend's *méchanceté* if they were alone. Scandal, gossip made tedious by morality, is only really enjoyable *en tête-à-tête*.

"I do so hope, Isabella, that you haven't had any more annoyance about the silly things that are being said about your pretty daughter-in-law," remarked Miss Westbury, leaning back with the comfortable amiability of a fat woman who expects to be amused.

Mrs. Wyburn looked round the room.

"Curious you never have your ceiling painted," she said. "I've often wondered why it is. It looks—you'll forgive me for saying so, Millie, won't you?—as if you left it in its present state from motives of, may I say, economy? But, of course, I know it isn't that—I always say, it's simply that you haven't noticed it. Thanks, no—no tea."

Miss Westbury's serenity was slightly disturbed, as her friend intended.

"I certainly don't spend my whole time lying on my back looking at the ceiling," she answered rather brusquely. "I have far too much to do."

"I never suggested that you should," quickly replied Mrs. Wyburn. "Such a thing never occurred to me for a single moment. And please don't think I wish to interfere, or to make remarks about anything that doesn't concern me. It merely struck me that if, at any time, you thought by some curious chance of having the house done up, it might be a pity to leave out the ceiling. But that was all. I do assure you, Millie, I never dreamt of hurting your feelings."

Miss Westbury laughed with a rather cackling sound—a sound Mrs. Wyburn recognised with satisfaction. It showed just the degree of slight annoyance she loved to cause in any one to whom she was speaking. Miss Westbury, however, waived the question and became hospitable.

"Do let me persuade you to have a toasted bun. Our baker makes them in a special way on purpose for me. There's nothing in the world more sensible with one's tea than a small toasted currant bun. I was speaking to Dr. Gribling about it only the other day, oddly enough, and he quite agreed with me."

"Why *only the other day?* and why *oddly enough*, Millie?—I dare say you speak to him constantly about it and about other equally urgent matters." She spoke with what she meant to be a slight sneer, in reply to which Miss Westbury behaved in a manner that is sometimes described as bridling up. She gave a movement meant to be a toss of the head and placed her lips firmly together.

"I like Dr. Gribling, Isabella, because he's a thoroughly sensible man—a man you can say anything to."

Mrs. Wyburn thought that Miss Westbury would say anything to any one, and she shrewdly suspected that Millie was probably the one gleam of amusement in poor old Dr. Gribling's dreary round. However, she waved the eminent physician aside and said—

"About Valentia. She and Romer have gone down to the country, you know."

"Oh, indeed! Quite early to go. Very nice. Have they a large party there, do you know? The Green Gate is such a charming place—so picturesque."

"Have you ever seen it?" Mrs. Wyburn asked.

"Only in the *Daily Mail*—I mean accounts of week-ends there, and that sort of thing. But I believe it's quite charming. It seems almost a pity though, doesn't it, at the end of the season to begin the same frivolities and gaieties all over again. I wonder they don't take a little rest."

"I believe they are resting. Valentia wrote to me that no one was staying there at all, except, of course, Daphne."

"And Harry de Freyne?"

"Yes, and Mr. de Freyne."

"Strange," said Miss Westbury comfortably. "Curious that extraordinary infatuation of your—son for this young man. But he's a very charming man, isn't he? Most agreeable?"

"He's not absolutely unpleasant."

"I suppose he brightens them up—amuses them? Probably he has very high spirits. Perhaps he has the *jar de veev*." Miss Westbury had a private pronunciation of foreign expressions all her own. "It is unfortunate, but do you know one often sees that in unprincipled people, Isabella."

"He knows that he's not quite a gentleman, and is trying to laugh it off," said Mrs. Wyburn.

"Does he really? Dear, dear—what a sad thing!—and yet he certainly *ought* to be a gentleman, you know. On his mother's side he is connected with the—"

"That's not the point," snapped Mrs. Wyburn. "And of course I don't mean to say that—outwardly—he's not. His manner and appearance are distinguished. It's the soul that's vulgar."

"Ah, I see! You mean you're afraid he isn't one of *nature's* gentlemen?"

"Nature? How do you mean? He has nothing to do with nature. He's a man about town."

"Oh, I beg your pardon—I understood he was an artist. And sometimes, you know, artists are extremely fond of nature; in fact, far *too* fond."

"I believe all that painting is only done to throw dust in people's eyes—an excuse for idleness. Candidly, I don't like studios; I don't think they're respectable."

"I know what you mean; but still, after all"—Miss Westbury made a feeble attempt at a good-natured defence—"after all, if they all like it—I mean to say, if they're all so happy, why should we—"

"I doubt if my son is happy."

"Oh, really, really? Do you think he's *ever noticed anything?* Isn't he devoted to Harry de Freyne?"

"Of course he hates him like poison," replied the mother.

Miss Westbury started in delighted horror, and replied sharply, "How do you know that? Did he tell you?"

"Tell me! He would never tell me. Besides, he couldn't tell me—he doesn't know it."

"And how do you know it?"

"Mothers know everything," she replied.

After a minute's pause, Miss Westbury said—

"But if you feel sure that Romer isn't happy, and that he, almost unconsciously perhaps, doesn't really like this young man being always about, mightn't it some day end in some trouble—some explosion?"

"It's quite possible."

"Then I wonder what Romer would do?"

"I know what he would do."

"Good heavens, Isabella, you don't mean to say that he would ever bring a—"

"It's really strange," said Mrs. Wyburn, "that at your age you should still be so silly. Will you never learn to understand anything at all? Of course not. He would protect her."

"Can't something be done? Why don't you speak to Valentia?"

"The advice of a relative-in-law in a case of this kind has never yet been known to be of any real use, Millie. I can only hope the whole thing may gradually wear itself out."

"May it be so, my dear!" echoed Miss Westbury, unctuously.

Mrs. Wyburn got up to go.

Miss Westbury helped her to fasten her mantle.

"I'm so glad you loosened it, or else you might not feel the benefit of it when you go out, Isabella," she observed, for she was not one to miss an opportunity of making a remark of this kind. "And *do* look on the bright side. I always say that things of this sort may not be true, and even if they are, everything may be for the best in the end."

Mrs. Wyburn liked to excite Millie's interest, and yet somehow loathed her sympathy.

"Yes; do you know, I really *should* have the ceiling painted, if I were you," she said, as if it were a new idea. "Otherwise your house is looking so nice—quite charming. I think it such an excellent plan not to have flowers in the windows, only ever-greens."

"So glad you think so. It *is* rather a good arrangement, because, you see, they always look exactly the same all the year round."

"That they certainly do—and nevergreens would be a better name for them," spitefully said Mrs. Wyburn to herself as she drove off.

"What a tiresome mood Isabella was in today," said Miss Westbury to herself. "I must go and see Jane Totness and tell her what she said. . . Ceiling, indeed! She *was* nasty!"

XX

A Proposal

M iss Luscombe was looking out of the window, looking up to the street, waiting. At last she saw from her basement (the "tank," as her friends called it) a glimpse on the pavement of a pair of feet that she knew. They were the feet of Mr. John Ryland Rathbone. She hastened to prepare herself for his visit.

It is obvious that people who live in a basement must look at life from a different point of view from all others. The proudest of women in that position must necessarily see it *de bas en haut*. The woman looking out of the drawing-room or higher for the person she is expecting to see gets more or less of a bird's-eye view. She sees the top of a hat first, and the person necessarily foreshortened. From the dining-room or ground-floor window she sees the approaching visitor through glass, but practically on a level, almost face to face, and therefore is incapable of judging him on the whole or of taking a very large view, since any object placed close to the eye deprives one of a sense of proportion— shuts out everything else. But from a basement window things are very different. It is wonderful how much character one learns to see in feet, and it is still more curious how, to the accustomed eye, their expression can vary from time to time. Flora saw at a glance by the obstinate stamp, the bad-tempered look of his boots, by the nervous impatience of his stride, that Mr. Rathbone was coming to see her in a state of agitation. One would hardly have believed that, without having seen his face at all, she would be so prepared for his behaviour when he arrived as to greet him anxiously from the door, even before he came in, with "Good heavens, what *is* the matter?"

"How do you know anything is the matter?"

"I guessed. I saw your steps."

"Everything is going wrong about the play. The expenses get larger every day. To sell even *one* ticket for a charity, they tell me, is simply out of the question! I must invite everybody, and even then most of them won't come. Just think, my dear Miss Luscombe, all this trouble, worry, and expense for amateurs to play *Romeo and Juliet* at an invitation performance to an absolutely empty house!"

"Why do you think it will be empty? . . . Your friends?"

"My friends? You're my only friend! Every chap at the Club I have spoken to about it said they would be out of town that day. One or two said they would come on afterwards and join me at supper. Supper! I said it was a *matinée*; so then they suggested I should give a dinner afterwards. And even women, they're quite as bad. I mentioned it to Lady Walmer. She is always so keen on going everywhere, and makes a hobby of odd charities and things. She said she was going yachting that day, and also that she was going to a wedding."

"What does it matter just about Lady Walmer?"

"Nothing, but it's an indication. Do we want to have no one in a theatre but the dressmakers who made the costumes? Miss Luscombe—Flora! I am beginning to think we'd better chuck it."

"Oh, Mr. Rathbone! The waste and the disappointment!"

"It would be a greater waste to make an utter fool of oneself in an empty house than to postpone it. I'm nervous. I'm really frightened. I'm beginning to see that I've been a fool. As to disappointment, *that*, Flora, you could console me for if you chose."

"Oh, Mr. Rathbone!"

"You really have been so sweet, so patient, it's my opinion that you are an angel!"

"Oh, indeed I'm not!"

"Well, you have the patience of one. You never think about yourself. You're all kindness and sweetness and thought for other people. To speak perfectly frankly, you have only one tiny fault, Flora. And that is, that you seem a *little* artificial. But it's my opinion that such affectations as you have are natural to you and you can't help them, and you would be an ideal wife."

Flora was actually silent with gratification. She did not even laugh.

"Look here, Flora, we'd better chuck the performance altogether. Let's give it up, and have a show instead at St. George's, Hanover Square."

"Are you making fun of me?" she asked, in a trembling voice, "because that would not be right. It wouldn't be nice of you—in fact, it would be rather cruel."

"You don't mean to say you care for me the least little bit?" He took both her hands and stared hard at her face. "Is there something real about you then?" he continued.

Tears came to her eyes. She turned her head away.

"This seems too good to be true," she murmured.

"Let's be married," he cried, "on the day we were going to have the show. Let's go to Oberammergau for our honeymoon, and don't let us ever go near the theatre again. Will you, dear? Or am I dreaming?"

"Of course. I always have," she answered ingenuously; "but I hadn't a scrap of hope, and I didn't know how much I cared for you."

"Dear Flora, I shall give up the stage and devote all my time to you."

"So will I," she said. "I shall never want to act again."

"Nor I, never—never!"

"I shall rush home and countermand everything," he cried.

"Oh, go not yet; it is not yet near day," she quoted in the tender voice she used for recitation.

He burst into peals of laughter, and put his arms round her and kissed her impetuously.

"Oh, Flora, what a fool I have been all this time! And you knew it—you knew it perfectly well. I thought when we were rehearsing that once you said the words, 'O Romeo, wherefore art *thou* Romeo?' with rather marked emphasis on the 'thou' . . ."

"Do you know that I never cared for any one but you in my life, Flora?"

"Oh, oh! Why is 'C. L.' tattooed on your wrist?"

"I'll have it taken out. I'll have Flora put on instead. I'll have anything you like tattooed in your honour—a hunting scene, a snap-shot of the Coronation—anything you like."

"No, please not. I don't like it; I can't bear it. It's the only thing I ever haven't liked about you. But we'll forget it now, won't we?" she said.

"And I'll forget the stage. Oh, Flora, how I have worried you! Forgive me. We won't think of anything but each other now."

They repeated this sentiment again and again in these and other words for about an hour and a half, and forgot to turn up lights and ring the bell.

THE FIRST REAL LOVE SCENE Flora had ever acted in was a triumphant success.

XXI

Hereford Vaughan

To have eleven plays, all written out of one's own head, and all being performed simultaneously in American, in Eskimo, and even in Turkish, besides in every known European language; to have money rolling in, and the strange world of agents and managers pursuing you by every post and imploring for more contracts by every Marconigram; and these triumphs to have come quite suddenly, was really enough to have turned the head of any young man; yet Hereford Vaughan's (known by his very few intimate friends as Gillie) had remained remarkably calm. He was not even embittered by success.

To know his jokes were being got over the footlights of so many lands was a curious sensation, and it often made him laugh suddenly to reflect how wicked certain quips must sound in, say, Japanese. Perhaps his friends were rather inclined to resent the way he retained his balance after what was really an almost unheard-of hit. They would have been readier to pardon it had he shown some sign of boring fatuity; or perhaps they thought he might at least have had a temporary nervous breakdown; taking the form (for choice) of losing all sense of the value of money and wildly throwing bank-notes and gold at every one he saw. But he remained quiet, reserved, and as apparently modest as ever.

Modesty is a valuable merit (as I think Schopenhauer has discovered) in people who have no other, and the appearance of it is extremely useful to those who have, but I am not suggesting that Vaughan was not human, and there was, no doubt, many a moment when he smiled to himself, and felt that he was a great man.

He was rather secretive and mysterious than blatant or dashing, and this, of course, made him, on the whole, more interesting to women. The fact that he had made a fortune and lived alone in a charming house with nothing but housekeepers, secretaries, telephones, typewriters, and cooks, of course made all the women of his acquaintance who had the match-making instinct (and what woman has not?) desire to see him married. As he showed no sign of doing so, they tried to console themselves by pretending that he had some secret romance. Old ladies hoped he had a broken heart for some fiancée who was lying under the daisies, having died of decline in the classical middle-Victorian way. Young ladies thought that he was probably fixed up in some way that would be sure in time to dissolve, and that he would marry later on. Far the most popular theory was that he didn't marry simply because he *was* married, privately; and that he had, no doubt, hurriedly espoused, before he was of age (and before the Registrar), some barmaid or chorus-girl, or other dreadful person, who had turned out far too respectable to divorce, and that he was thus a young man marred. They had no grounds for the rumour except that clever and promising young men often did these things, and he had always been a particularly promising young man, and in this unfortunate case had probably kept his promise.

Vaughan was sitting one morning reading his notices (never believe the greatest men when they tell you that they don't do that!), when Muir Howard came cheerily, almost boisterously, into the room. He was an old school friend who had been devoted to Gillie long before his arrival, and of whose faults, virtues, cheeriness, and admiration Vaughan had made a confirmed habit.

Muir was a very good-looking barrister, with vague parliamentary ambitions and a definite love of machinery. He always had pink cheeks, and wore a pink carnation, and looked as flourishing, gay, and yet, somehow, battered, as Vaughan looked pale, fresh, and sardonic. One of the things that surprised the general public was that Vaughan could not live without the continuous society of a person who certainly could not understand a word he wrote or much that he said. They didn't realise that Vaughan was so accustomed to not listening to Muir's long confidences, to disputing every proposition he made, and contradicting every word he said, that he always felt lost when his friend was away. Muir regarded him as a combination of hero, genius, pet, and child, and was always giving him advice and imploring him not to do too much. To Vaughan he was, as I have said, a habit, and there is always something agreeable in a habit of which one is a little tired.

He had arrived this morning on his bicycle, and came in bringing a whiff of heartiness, self-complacency, and fresh air, saying, "Hallo! hallo! hallo! Priceless to find you in, Gillie!" All he got for it was that Vaughan looked up and said—

"You used to be only breezy. Now you're becoming a thorough draught. Fold up and keep quiet, can't you?"

"Nervous, I suppose," said Muir, in a sympathetic voice. "I wonder you don't take that stuff that you see in the papers about what is good for—"

"Sudden pains in the back on washing-day, bending over the tub, and so forth? The portraits of the people before taking the remedy and after decided me. It seems, by the pictures, to make your hair grow long and give you whiskers and a ghastly squint. Ruins your clothes, too. Your collars get the wrong shape."

"Oh well, leave it alone, then. Perhaps you're right. . . You haven't asked me about the Walmers' dance. I took Miss de Freyne to supper. The American chap never turned up, and I was getting on with her simply rippingly, when *what* do you think she said? Confided in me that she was privately engaged to and frightfully keen on that boy you met at Harry's. The baby Guardsman. Isn't it sickening?"

"What did Miss Walmer do?" asked Vaughan.

"She sort of hung about, waiting for Harry, who seemed to be getting on all right with the two strings to his bow, or two stools, or two bundles of hay, or whatever it is. What luck some people have!"

"Not in this case. He'll lose them both."

"Really? Why?"

"He's not a diplomatist, and he wants such a lot for himself. He wants too much. No self-restraint."

"Pretty useless for Mrs. Wyburn. I like her. She looked topping last night, too. But I dare say it'll be all right. Romer's a good chap. Awfully dull."

"Most interesting. Are you going to stay here much longer, Muir?"

"Why? Yes."

Vaughan got up.

"All right. Do. I'm going out."

"Where?"

Vaughan did not answer, but gave the heap of notices to his friend, and said—

"Just divide the sheep and goats for me, will you? That's just what they are, the critics—either sheep or goats."

"Of course I will. But, I say—I came here to have a talk."

"I know you did. You have talked."

He went out. Muir smiled to himself, enjoying this treatment as an eccentricity of genius.

Five minutes later Gillie came back.

XXII

GILLIE INTERFERES

He was not much surprised to find Muir proudly examining the invitation cards on the mantelpiece. Muir started and turned round as he came in.

"Back again? Capital!"

"Well, of all the snobs!" said Vaughan.

"Hang it, Gillie, it's only for you. I'm pleased you're getting on, that's all."

"No words can tell you how I despise your point of view. Just tell me something I want to know. Wasn't there a sort of little scene at this dance last night?"

"I didn't see anything," he answered.

"You never do."

"Oh, I remember now, I heard something. It appears that Romer left his wife and Daphne at the dance and then came back in an hour to fetch them, and she wasn't there."

"Who wasn't where?"

"Val and Harry had gone for a little fresh air in a taxi for about a quarter of an hour, that's all. They came back and explained it."

"They would. Don't apologise."

"But just the few minutes that Romer was looking for them made—well, rather a fuss. It was perfectly all right afterwards. They all had supper together. So there wasn't much talk about it, except, as I say, while Romer was waiting for them. I never in my life saw any one look so ghastly as that chap did."

Vaughan sat down and looked thoughtful.

"Only you, Muir, would leave out the only thing of the slightest importance that you had to tell me, which I hear the second I leave the house from that round-faced tattooed idiot, Rathbone, at the corner of the street."

"But I tell you it's all right, old chap."

"All right? Don't you see that this sort of thing constantly happening will gradually undermine. . . ? I like Valentia. It's a great shame."

"Harry certainly isn't worth smashing up a happy home for," Muir answered, "if that's what you're afraid of. But. . . when he marries

Miss Walmer it'll be all right. Val will forget about him, and settle down with Romer again. I'm deeper than you think, Gillie. . . ah, I don't say much, but I can see as far through a brick wall as most people!"

"Just about as far, I should think," said Vaughan contemptuously.

"What do you propose to do about it?"

"It's likely I'd tell you." Gillie sat down to his desk and rang a bell.

"I suppose I've got to go now, eh?"

"Almost time, I should think."

"Ha, ha, ha! Capital! Well, so long! Be good."

Muir went away as heartily as he had arrived.

The bell was answered by the entrance of the housekeeper, Mrs. Mills. She was a muddle-headed, elderly woman in black silk, whom Vaughan kept because her extraordinary tactlessness amused him. She invariably managed to do and say the wrong thing at the right time. Today it was a hot morning in July. She came in holding in her hand a little card covered with frost and robins.

"Mr. Vaughan, sir, I appened to be going through my things, and I come across this, sir. I thought pre-aps you'd like it. It is pretty."

She insisted on his taking it.

"Charming, Mrs. Mills, but I don't quite see—"

"Oh, look at the words, sir! They're what I call so appropriate! Do read them."

He read the beautiful words—

Wishing you a blithe and gladsome Yule.

"What on earth—?"

"Well, sir, I only thought they was pretty, and pre-aps you'd like to keep it, sir, or send it to one of your young ladies; but I'll take it away if you don't like it." She put it back in her pocket.

"Frankly, I don't. What a genius you have for the wrong thing! Are you going to give me plum pudding and turkey on Midsummer Day?"

"I shouldn't dream of such a thing, sir."

Gillie had scribbled a letter.

"Go and ring up a messenger boy, will you?"

"May I send Johnson, sir? I don't old with telephones. They buzz at you or makes you jump. And the young person keeps on saying ave you got them? before you've ad time to breathe, in a manner of speaking."

She took the note. Vaughan sat down on a sofa to wait for the answer, glanced at the clock, and said, "Confound Muir! He's made me waste another morning."

When the answer came, Gillie went out and strolled towards Mount Street.

He found Valentia at home, evidently flattered and fluttered at seeing him.

"How sweet of you to come!" she said.

"You'll stay to lunch, of course?"

"I'm afraid I can't."

"Oh! lunching with a leading lady, I suppose?"

"No."

"With whom?"

"With Romeike and Curtice."

"Not really? What fun! What are they like?"

"Oh, Romeike is all right. I don't care so much about Curtice."

She gave him a cigarette.

"I never in my life," said Vaughan, "before today, attempted to interfere in anybody else's affairs."

She stared at him.

"But in this case it—may I really smoke?—does seem such a pity! Of course you know what I mean, don't you?"

"Do I?"

"You see, I feel so certain that if you were, let's say—married to *Harry* and met Romer after, you'd be so wildly in love with Romer."

"So I was," she said in a low voice. "Tremendously! I thought he was a strong silent man with a great deal in him. . . Oh! I've told you."

"Yes, but so he is. It's commonplace of you, really, Val, not to see it."

"I'm awfully sorry. . . I do love Romer, and I think I appreciate him. But somehow it's a little dull. It's not exciting as I thought it would be."

"Well! if you *must* have fun, and amusement, and make a hero of somebody, why just Harry? Why not a superior man? Me, for instance?"

He was laughing.

"I've been told that an adoration for you would be hopeless, utterly hopeless." She smiled. "And we're friends. I can't imagine—"

"Nor I. Of course I know it's utterly absurd to come and give people advice on these subjects, and one can't dispute about tastes and all that. But my practical mind revolts to see any one so delightful as you throwing away the substance for the shadow. You see, I'm a mass of platitudes."

"Shadows are very attractive sometimes."

"But they go away too. And then where are you?"

She was silent.

"They do, really. I know what I'm talking about." He stood up. "Think over what I've said."

"You're kind, but you're rather depressing, Gillie," said Val. She looked a little frightened, but very pretty.

"When do you go back to the country?"

"Oh, today. We're there now. We only came up for the dance. We're motoring down to the Green Gate. . . All of us."

"Oh yes. . . I'm afraid you must think me very impertinent."

"Indeed I don't."

"And when I've gone you will give orders that you're never at home to me again. But, somehow, I couldn't help it. If it makes you hate me to remember what I've said, forget it."

She laughed as he rose to go.

"That's all right, Gillie; but what I want to know is, where you're really going."

"I'll tell you, exactly. I'm going home to lunch, because I've an urgent appointment immediately afterwards."

"More plays, I suppose? What sort this time?"

"A light comedy, with a very slight love interest," he answered, "all dialogue, no action. . . At least, so far."

"Oh, then it isn't finished yet?"

"Not quite. Good-bye. And if you ever want a change, remember—a *superior* man!"

They both laughed insincerely.

He left her looking thoughtfully out of the window.

XXIII

The Bald-Faced Stag

Vaughan went home, and after lunching, chiefly on a newspaper and a cup of coffee, he got into a taxicab and gave a direction.

The vehicle flew smoothly along down Park Lane, past the Marble Arch into the Edgware Road, and on from there between houses and shops, growing gradually uglier and uglier, to Maida Vale, up Shoot-up Hill, and so on until there was a glimpse of suburban country, and gasworks, and glaring posters of melodramas on hoardings, till it stopped suddenly at a real little old roadside inn, straight out of Dickens—"The Bald-faced Stag at Edgware." Edgware suggested *John Gilpin*, Gillie's favourite poem.

Here he got out, and was positively welcomed, and heartily, by a real roadside innkeeper—also out of Dickens—resembling the elder Weller—a local magnate called Tom Brill, who looked a relic of the coaching days, though really he never did anything but stand in front of the inn in his shirt-sleeves and welcome people.

Vaughan, obviously an habitué, walked through the inn into a perfectly adorable garden, which was so large, so quiet, and so full of pinks, hollyhocks, and other old-fashioned flowers, so absolutely peaceful and sleepy, that one could have imagined oneself miles away in the country.

The garden belonged as much to the Dickens period as the inn itself. It contained a great many wooden arbours in which one could imagine ladies in crinolines archly accepting tea, or refusing sips of shrub (whatever that may be) with whiskered gentlemen. There was a large cage full of Persian pheasants with gorgeous Indian colouring, which always suggested to Vaughan—he didn't know why—the Crimean War. There was a parlour covered with coloured prints of racehorses and boxing matches, and in which was a little round table painted as a draught-board, and furnished with a set of Indian chessmen of red and white ivory. The whole thing, though only twenty minutes' drive from Mayfair, was unknown, unspoilt, and apparently had not altered in any particular since about 1856. Its great charm was that it was utterly unself-conscious; it had no idea that it was quaint.

Vaughan sat down on a rustic seat and plunged into the atmosphere of the period that he loved, revelling in the soothing, delightful calm, and in the fact that nobody there knew who he was (though they knew him well by name), and that none of his friends and acquaintances would have dreamt that he was there.

A large field beyond the garden contained cows, hay, and other rustic things.

Presently Tom Brill came up to him, and he asked after Mrs. Brill, whom her husband always described, with confidential pride, as "Though I say it that shouldn't say it, as fine a woman as you'll meet in a day's march."

Vaughan always assented to this proposition. As he had never himself in his life been for a day's march, and probably never would, he certainly would have had no right to contradict Mr. Brill on the subject.

"Is Miss Brill at home?" he presently asked. "May I see her?"

"Certainly, sir, of course you shall. She's helping her mother. I'll call her. Don't move, sir, don't move."

Miss Brill, who had been helping her mother to look out of the window, now came into the garden, which immediately became idyllic.

She was not in any way like the innkeeper's daughter of Comic Opera. She was a schoolgirl of sixteen, with a long, fair plait, a short serge skirt, and a seraphic oval face. She ought to have been called Fanny or Clara. Unluckily her name was Gladys.

She said in a very sweet voice—

"You're quite a stranger, sir." And she amplified the assertion by adding, "You haven't been here not this ever so long."

"I know I haven't, but I've been longing to come."

"Not you!" she said ironically.

She was standing opposite him, with her hands behind her back. Without a hat, in the glaring afternoon sun, with the complexion, pale pink and white, of a china doll that had never made up, she was a refreshing sight after the theatrical world in London, not to speak of society. Vaughan seemed to think so.

"Well, how did you enjoy the play?" he asked.

"It was very kind of you to send us the tickets. Mother enjoyed it."

"You didn't care much for the piece yourself?"

"I thought it was rather silly," she answered.

He had never had a criticism on his work that pleased him more.

"I mean," she went on, "I shouldn't have thought—well, nobody would go on like that."

"Go on how?"

"Why, go on so silly."

"You wouldn't like to see another play, written by the same man, then?"

"I wouldn't mind another one. Wild horses wouldn't drag me to see that again."

"Wild horses are not likely to try," he observed. At which jest she laughed loudly and charmingly, showing marvellous teeth. She had no cockney accent, though she occasionally and fitfully dropped an H.

"Oh, Gladys, do take me for a walk in the field."

"Want to see the calf?"

"No; I can live without seeing the calf. I want to sit in the field with you."

"You are a caution! Come on then, but I can't stay long."

They climbed the gate, which she seemed to think a quicker mode of entrance than sending for the key, and sat in the field, from which Mr. Brill always declared you could see three counties. Perhaps you could; if so, they all looked exactly alike.

"It's quiet here, isn't it? I shan't have much more of it," she remarked.

"Oh, Gladys! Don't say you're going away!"

"Of course I am. Don't you know I'm going to be a manicure in Bond Street?"

"Bond Street? How revolting! Is that your ambition?"

"Why, I think it would be very nice. I must do something. Father's settled about it. First I'm going to pay to learn it, and then I shall earn quite a lot. It's a great hairdresser's."

"I think it's horrible, Gladys. Perhaps you'll fall in love with a German hairdresser, and be lost to me for ever."

"I shan't fall in love with no foreigners, don't you fret."

"I'm not fretting. Will you have your hair done up?" he asked, lifting the long plait.

"Well, of course I shall, and waved, and that."

"Gladys, they'll spoil you."

The conversation went on in this strain for some time. She alternately repeated the exclamation, "How you do go on!" or accused him of the mysterious crime of being a caution, but she never stopped looking perfectly beautiful and seraphic.

When they went back to the garden a few other visitors had straggled in. They all seemed to come in high dog-carts, and they always ordered eggs, jam, and watercress with their tea, and were immensely impressed by the Persian pheasants.

Vaughan went back to London feeling refreshed, and already, strangely, counting the days till he could come back.

There was not a woman in the world he knew whom he would have taken the slightest trouble to see except Gladys, the innkeeper's daughter. She was an illiterate schoolgirl; and though she had a lovely face, she was stupid, and probably not so angelic as she looked; but he always felt a little disappointed as he drove back. He wished she were in love with him.

And this ungratified wish was, in all his full life with its brilliant success, perhaps his greatest real pleasure.

XXIV

The Green Gate

When Harry came down to breakfast, a little late, he found Valentia waiting to pour out his coffee, and some letters on his plate. She watched him as he opened them. Most of them looked like bills. On the envelope of one was a little blue flag. Harry put this letter in his pocket, and went on eating.

"It's a lovely morning, Harry. So fresh; just the sort of day not to do anything at all."

"Ah! that's what's so delightful about you all," he answered. "You never say, 'What shall we do?' and neither of you have ever said yet that this is Liberty Hall, which means, as a rule, in a country house, 'Breakfast at eight o'clock sharp, you won't mind it being a little cold if you're late, and then we are going for a motor drive at 9.30.' Still, I think, perhaps, one ought to take a little exercise. I feel almost equal to a game of croquet this afternoon—later on—when I'm stronger. Is any one coming down today?"

"No. And only Van Buren, and Vaughan and Muir Howard on Sunday. I see you've heard from the Walmers. What do they say?"

"It's sure to be nothing of interest. How I love your hair parted on one side! It makes you look like a boy."

"Not a principal boy, I hope. Why not read the letter?"

Harry got up and fetched himself something from the sideboard.

"I don't feel quite strong enough yet. When I've had breakfast. I should like to paint you as you're looking now, Val. I think I'll do a sketch of you in the rose garden, all in black and white, like a Beardsley, with the balustrades and steps and things behind you. Will you sit to me?"

"That's all very well. But why don't you read your letter?"

"There's sure to be nothing in it."

"How can you tell till you've opened it?"

"I know. I always feel what's in a letter without opening it. Don't you? I absorb the essence, as it were, through the covers of the envelope, as somebody or other—Macaulay, I think—used to absorb all the important things through the covers of a book. Or wasn't it Macaulay?

Anyhow, it doesn't matter. It was some tiresome person whom one oughtn't to talk about on a morning like this."

Harry evidently was not quite at his ease.

"But why not read it?" She spoke playfully.

"How persistent women are, just like children. To tease you I just shan't."

"Oh, Harry!"

"I shan't read it now at all," he went on. "I can answer it without reading it."

"It's only that I should like to know how the Walmers are enjoying themselves on *Flying Fish*. Lady Walmer was a little afraid they mightn't like it."

Here Romer came up to the window and called out—

"I say, Val, come here a minute. I want to ask you something."

"Here I am, dear," and she vanished into the garden.

The second she had gone Harry opened the letter very carefully, and read—

Dearest Harry,

"You are a rotter never to write. I'm having *such* a time. Weather priceless, but very sick at not hearing from you. Algie Thynne is here. Do you know him? He's rather a nut. Wish you were here. No more today. Bye-bye, old son.

Your loving
ALEC

"P.S.—Do write. The moonlight nights are simply topping. Just like a picture. I think you'd like it; otherwise everything is beastly.

"I love you more than ever.

A

He put the letter back in the untorn envelope and carefully fastened it up again. He then placed it on the mantelpiece, and having finished his breakfast, lit a cigarette.

He looked thoughtful.

"Algie Thynne, indeed!" he said to himself. "How pathetic, trying to make me jealous! Well, it's a pretty letter, and what's more, it must be answered."

Val came back.

"Romer wants the lawn mown," she said. "He's perfectly mad on the subject of mowing the lawn. He seems to think it ought to be shaved every day. It's the only thing he knows about the country. Well, have you read your letter?"

"There it is," said Harry. "You can read it if you like." He watched her carefully as she took it from the mantelpiece.

"I don't want to read it," she said, holding it.

"Nor do I," said Harry.

"Harry, tell me honestly, wouldn't you really mind if I tore it into little bits and put it in the waste-paper basket—just as it is?"

"Not a straw," said Harry, shaking his head.

She clapped her hands, tore it into tiny pieces, and threw it in the basket. Then she said, in a low voice of deep gratitude—

"Oh, Harry, you are sweet! Do forgive me."

"I don't see that there's anything to forgive," said Harry.

"Yes, there is; lots. I'm afraid I've been horrid. I'll never bother you about any thing again."

She was simply beaming.

"Good," answered Harry indifferently.

But as he followed her into the garden he looked rather perplexed. He felt that this sort of thing was not leading up very well to what he would have to tell her soon. However, why spoil a lovely day by thinking of it?

Like a schoolboy with his holiday task before him, he put it off as long as possible.

Though he didn't own it to himself, and was disdainfully amused at Alec's letter, still the thought of Algie Thynne, moonlight nights on the yacht, topping weather, and his own neglect, gave him some cause for alarm. Algie Thynne was *criblé* with debts, and probably keen on marrying for money. Contemptible young ass! Why didn't he *work*? Harry despised him.

At the earliest opportunity (which, by the way, did not arise until he had made an excuse to go into the village, where he wrote at the post office) the answer was sent.

Even Harry found the beginning of the letter too difficult, so he always began (as Valentia might have said) without a beginning, which impressed Miss Walmer much more. Ever since he had reached the age of discretion, which, in his case, was at his majority, Harry had been thoroughly trained in the habit of writing letters that gratified the recipient enormously without compromising the writer in the slightest degree. The habitual dread of those *bêtes noires* of Don Juan—the breach of promise case and the Divorce Court—had got him into the way of writing the sort of letter that he would have had no objection to hear read aloud in court. Perhaps that was why the sentences were always polished, and the meaning a little vague.

". . . I don't speak your language, perhaps, but I understand your letter, reading between the lines. It came like a whiff of fresh sea air. Yes, it would be delightful to be on board *Flying Fish* now. However, no doubt Algie Thynne—(*how* eloquently, by the way, you describe him! putting all the complications of his character and the dazzling charm of his personality in a nutshell by the simple sentence '*He's rather a nut!*')—amply compensates for my absence. You ask if I know him. I do, though perhaps more by reputation than anything else. We have met once or twice. Where? I can't quite recall. Perhaps at the Oratory, or at the Supper Club or some place of that sort. But somehow I never pursued his acquaintance, nor did it ever ripen into friendship. I felt, instinctively, that he was too clever for me.

"I trust all the same that his brilliance will not altogether overshadow your memory of *others*. I should not like to think that we were drifting apart. Still, if it should be so, I must resign myself. I could still be happy in thinking of you, Alec.

> *'Love that is love at all*
> *Asks for no earthly coronal'*—

but, I remember, you once expressed to me your opinion that *all poetry is rot*. So I will not bore you with quotations. It is pleasant here, and my cousins are very kind, and leave me alone to think as much as I like. I'm not, somehow, quite in the mood for the usual gaieties and frivolities of a country house. Last night we played Musical Chairs until two in the morning, and today I am a little weary. Your postscript gave me joy. I need not say that I reciprocate it, need I? . . .

"I feel all that you are feeling, and somehow even know what you are doing, and if you did not write again until we meet, I should not be anxious. I have a trusting nature. But when you wire, remember that the telegraph boy has a good way to walk, and when telegrams arrive after midnight, it causes a sensation and much inquiry. Also I cannot help feeling that every one in the village, as well as at the Green Gate, has read the words I would like to keep to myself alone. I have a curious love of mystery—isn't mystery the great charm of all romance?—So to gratify this fancy of mine, sign your next telegram 'Johnson.' I know you won't mind.

"When we meet again, all, I trust, will be clear and definite before us. Best love to dear Lady Walmer, and to yourself what I am sure you will know. Don't be angry with me for not writing oftener. I find it very difficult to express my thoughts, for alas, I have no command of language. Not only that, the pens here have one great fault—they won't write. Otherwise they're quite excellent. . . Yes, your note has given me, as the French say, 'furiously to think.'

"Hoping that all will go well with you, and looking forward, think me as always,

Yours, faithfully,
HARRY BROKE DE FREYNE

"There! that ought to keep her quiet for a month," he thought as he posted the letter, and with a sigh of relief turned back towards the Green Gate.

XXV

A Sunday Afternoon

By this time Van Buren was entirely in Harry's confidence; that is to say, Harry had gradually trained him to bear without flinching the situation as Harry represented it. He believed Harry had a hopeless romantic affection for Mrs. Romer Wyburn which he was trying to stifle, and that Miss Walmer being hopelessly in love with *him*, he was doing his best to marry her, partly, as he candidly admitted, on worldly grounds.

Van Buren was deeply touched at Harry's trust in him, and was always trying to keep him up to his good resolutions by pointing out that any understanding (however Platonic) between the pretty Valentia and the handsome guest was dishonourable, a breach of hospitality towards Romer, that silent but admirable host.

Indeed, he repeated to Harry so often and so firmly, "It can't be done; one can't make love to the wife of a friend," that Harry was driven to the point of replying that he hardly saw whom else, as a matter of fact, one *could* very well make love to; it being impossible to have romances with people one didn't know. And in this case the fact that Harry was very fond of Romer made the temptation far greater, as he explained; Harry being (as he pointed out) so very sensitive and highly strung that he could never, somehow, be really attracted by a woman whose husband was not sympathetic to him. Which point of view Van Buren, shaking his head, regarded as unsound.

Harry now spent much time giving picturesque sketches and impressions of his feelings to his friend, for he had an almost feminine love of talking over personal affairs to the sympathetic. In his benevolence Van Buren longed to protect Valentia and Romer, and to give Miss Walmer all she wanted; but most of all his idea was to save Harry from himself, so he always accepted with alacrity invitations to the Green Gate for altruistic reasons. Besides, his desire to see Daphne, although she was now becoming more and more remote to him, was still persistent, if a little less vivid.

"I've had a beautiful womanly letter from Alec today," Harry confided in Van as soon as he arrived. "You know the sort of thing she writes: all in jerks and subaltern's slang. With sincere sentiment showing between the lines. And I answered it."

"A beautiful manly letter, I hope? I'm sure you could do that as well as any one, Harry."

Harry smiled.

"Oh, just some vague, cautious slosh, not unamusing in its way—it'll *get* there all right."

"Yes, Harry, I know, but I do hope—Ah, Miss Daphne, how beautiful your England is looking today! In America we never have a day like this, warm and yet cool, with all those nice, white, fleecy clouds in the sky. Our atmosphere is always so hard and clear. Now this garden with those large trees is just like a Corot. They *are* fine trees. Poplars, I presume?"

"You *do* presume," smiled Daphne; "I don't know what they are, but I'm perfectly sure they're not poplars."

"Oh yes—I'm wrong. They're oaks, I've no doubt." He hummed, "'The oak and the ash and the bonny ivy tree.' Do let's walk over and look at them closer, Miss Daphne."

"I'm afraid I can't. Tea's ready."

To his annoyance Van was obliged to follow Daphne and join the group round the tea-table. He declined with some formality of manner to accept the glass of iced water Daphne offered him, and looked at her with that look of tender, fixed, respectful reproach that had the effect of irritating her very nearly to the point of incivility.

She turned to Muir Howard, who was looking very pink and cheery. Muir was a popular man for his great ease in making conversation, the kind that is as the pudding part in a plum pudding, and without which the plums, however delightful, could hardly stick together. Though the great majority of people talk commonplaces, their banalities are by no means always the kind that help. Muir's particular way of opening open doors, flogging dead horses, and genially enjoying any spark of fun in his friends, coupled with his good looks and pleasant, hearty disposition, made him a most useful and welcome guest, as a sort of super. He was quite decorative, and could be turned on to talk newspaper politics to dull men, pretty platitudes to plain women; to make himself generally useful, and altogether to help things to go. In this way he was invaluable. Young girls always liked him; he was a great favourite with elderly ladies, and with men of his own age also, who were, however, occasionally bored with his worship for his friend

Vaughan. He found it very difficult not to mention Gillie less than once in every five minutes.

That distinguished young man, who was beginning to look a little jaded with incense, was engrossed with his hostess. Whenever he was there Harry always became particularly devoted in his manner to Valentia, and scarcely ever left her other side. This was one of the reasons that she enjoyed Gillie's presence, besides that she was, now that she knew him well, particularly fond of him. His conversation and personality in general had a special flavour.

Every one was talking and laughing with the light intoxication produced by tea and cigarettes in the open air on a fine Sunday afternoon, excepting only Romer, who as usual said hardly anything, absorbed in admiration of his wife. He suddenly remarked—

"I say, Val. The Campbells are coming."

He wondered why this statement produced a burst of irresponsible laughter.

"What fun! Will there be bagpipes?" Vaughan asked.

"No, no. Romer means the Prebendary Campbell, or at least his wife and daughter. They're coming to see us this afternoon. I had quite forgotten. Please all behave nicely. They've been a long time making up their minds. I believe they think we're frivolous."

"Not really? How could they? It reminds one of the story of Henry James." Vaughan stopped to light a cigarette.

"Go on."

"It appears that for some time his near neighbours in the country looked a little coldly on him on the grounds that, being a writer, he must be Bohemian. At last the local doctor's wife and clergyman's wife called on him, and finding him perfectly respectable, stayed for many hours. They were particularly tedious and rather self-righteous. When they had gone, he said thoughtfully to some one who was pitying him for being bored, 'One of those poor wantons has a certain cadaverous grace.'"

The story was well received, except by Van Buren, who seemed painfully shocked.

Daphne, who had gone into the house to fetch some snapshots, now came running back saying—

"Val, Val! The Campbells are arriving in a fly, and they seem to have brought their foreigner with them—that man Miss Campbell told me about. He's a kind of Belgian, and awfully clever—he's invented something."

"What's he invented?"

"Brussels sprouts?" suggested Harry rather sleepily.

"But they've been invented already."

"Why shouldn't he invent them over again? Give him a chance."

Muir began to sing softly, "Young Lochinvar has come out of the West," which he appeared to think a suitable serenade, but he stopped suddenly at Gillie's entreaty.

"I don't mind anything Muir does, as long as he doesn't sing," he always explained.

"It's awful hard lines. I've got a ripping baritone voice, but I never have a chance to use it," murmured Muir.

"You shall sing to me this afternoon. I'll accompany you," whispered Daphne.

Muir had gratefully answered that it was frightfully decent of her, when the servant announced—

"Mrs. and Miss Campbell. Mr.—" He left a blank, unable to pronounce the name.

But Mrs. Campbell introduced Mynheer von Stoendyck.

Mrs. Campbell was an amiable, colourless woman, with a greyish brown fringe that looked as if it were made of Berlin wool. Though she was not yet forty-five, she wore a bonnet with violet velvet strings, and had a very long waist. Also, her skirt, in reality quite normal, looked, to the eye used to contemporary fashion, grotesquely wide at the end.

Her daughter was an ordinary Rectory girl, spoilt by a dash of culture. At a glance all present saw she was in love with Mr. Stoendyck. He was a well-set-up man of about thirty-five, with a military manner and scientific eye-glasses, also a turned-up light moustache. He spoke all languages with one rasping accent, but Mrs. Campbell seemed to suffer under the delusion that he could only understand broken English. So whenever people spoke to him she translated their remarks into a sort of baby language that seemed singularly out of place from her.

"I'm afraid you must think me dreadfully worldly, calling on you on a Sunday," said Mrs. Campbell, laughing socially as she sat down. "But what the Prebendary always says is, the better the day the better the deed."

"Oh, does he always say that?" Harry asked with great apparent interest, waking up. He had been overpowered with languor ever since lunch.

"Yes, and I felt sure you wouldn't mind our bringing our friend, Mr. Stoendyck. He is so clever. He's come over to England about an invention."

Val thought of Brussels sprouts, but did not suggest it.

Mrs. Campbell apparently couldn't take her eyes off the Belgian, whom she watched as one watches a rather dangerous pet, though he appeared particularly safe.

Muir, for an unknown reason addressing the Belgian as Professor, was asking him his impressions of England. Mrs. Campbell bent forward, and said with a nod—

"E ope you like it—Angleterre, you know"—and nodded idiotically.

"I find it most interesting," said Mr. Stoendyck raspingly, in admirable English. "There are opportunities in this country for the pursuance of science, art, and social intercourse which one would hardly have expected. I do not take tea, I thank you much."

"Have a glass of beer?" said Romer, suddenly inspired.

Simple as the sentence was, Mrs. Campbell thought it necessary to translate it with more nods.

"E ask you, ave beer. *Bière*, you know! Glass," and then she went on in her usual tone, "Most thoughtful of Mr. Wyburn, I'm sure. What a charming place this is of yours, Mrs. Wyburn. I always say the Green Gate is the most picturesque place in the neighbourhood. And Mr. de Freyne, I understand, is an artist. Do you know my daughter, Marion, is *so* interested in art! And my younger son, Garstin, though he is only twelve years old, shows great artistic talent, too. He did a map of Buckinghamshire that really surprised me, almost any one would recognise it at a glance. I always say I'm sure some day Garstin will be in the Royal Academy."

Van Buren had approached and began to talk to Mrs. Campbell. Val went over to the Belgian, but she heard the American beginning a sentence as usual with, "Pleased to meet you. I've never had the opportunity of mixing much in clerical circles in New York, Mrs. Campbell," and felt sure he was going to ask impossible questions about Prebendaries and Rural Deans.

The rasping Belgian, on whom both the mother and daughter cast continual anxious and admiring eyes, though he seemed thoroughly able to take care of himself, said to Muir, who was taking him on—

"No, I do not spend my entire time over my invention. Mrs. Campbell is so kind as to take me for drives in the environment, to give me a right impression of the beauties of Hertfordshire. For relaxation I play the piano."

"Ha! Musical, eh, Professor?" asked Muir shrewdly. "That's right; so am I. I'm awfully keen on music." He spoke reassuringly.

Mr. Stoendyck looked at him through his glasses, and said without interest—

"Indeed. I find Beethoven's Fifth Symphony, even on the piano, extraordinarily satisfying and refreshing to the mind after the strain of looking at English scenery." He drank a long draught of iced lager.

"Oh! Classical, eh? I'm not up to that. Queen's Hall, eh? That sort of thing."

"I beg your pardon? Is there—Has the Queen a hall in this neighbourhood?"

"How do you mean, Professor?"

"What do you say?"

"I beg your pardon?"

Mrs. Campbell, who managed to hear through her own conversation with Van Buren, called out—

"E say e no understand," and nodded smilingly, seeming to think she had helped matters considerably.

Miss Campbell talked of tennis, matins, hats and the opera to Daphne, but appeared to be absent, and occasionally smiled at the foreigner, who ignored her.

At last the Campbells and their Belgian withdrew, Mrs. Campbell saying that the Prebendary wished them to go to Evensong. Their departure left, as such visits do, a blank and a reaction. Our friends were silent for a minute.

Then Vaughan said—

"I feel crushed, and a little flattened out, too."

"*I* feel as if my brain were made of cotton wool," said Harry.

"Come and sing," suggested Daphne to Muir, and they went off to the drawing-room, from which strains were soon heard about *It Is not because*,—something or other.

In the middle of the song Daphne played a wrong note, stopped, and said—

"Oh, I wish Cyril was here!"

"So do I. If he can accompany, I wish he was here."

"Oh, go on!"

"It Is not because thy heart is mine" . . .

THE PARTY IN THE GARDEN listened with a worried expression.

"How about croquet?" suggested Val. "The tapping noise will take it off."

"Yes. Come on."

"You can't," said Romer. "The lawn wants mowing."

XXVI

In the Rose Garden

"H ow lovely this place must look at dawn!"

"By Jove! That's an idea, Gillie," said Harry. "It must look glorious."

They were sitting in the rose garden with Valentia. It was still quite light, though the sunset glow had nearly faded. There was a rich mellow tone in the sky, a promise of peace, a feeling that it was the end of the day, which, combined with the almost cloyingly sweet scent of the roses, was enough to make any one feel poetical.

"To think we've never seen the sun rise here!" exclaimed Valentia.

Romer here joined them, smoking a cigarette.

"Hasn't Romer ever seen the sun rise here?" Vaughan asked.

"Never," said Romer.

"Why not?"

"I don't know. I suppose because it always happens after I've gone to bed," he answered drily.

"Let's sit up all night and see it tomorrow," suggested Valentia.

"Yes. Capital! Do let us!" said Harry.

Romer did not appear much taken with this scheme.

"Oh no, you mustn't *sit* up," said Vaughan. "That's not the way to see it."

"Is there so much difference between staying up and getting up then?" Val asked.

"Yes, indeed, all the difference in the world. You must get up fresh, with the birds."

"What time do birds get up? Is it *very* early?"

"It would do if you were out at three this time of the year, or even at four."

"Well, let's do it!"

"Oh, I don't think I shall," said Harry.

He looked at Valentia.

She answered—

"You might make a sketch, you know, of the early birds getting up to catch the worms. But—I don't think I shall. Anyhow, not *tomorrow* at *half-past three*."

"All right," said Harry with a nod, "we won't. Don't tell Daphne, or she'll be out at 3.15 to the tick, to take a snapshot of the dawn."

"A snapshot of the dawn! Wouldn't that be sacrilege?"

"Young girls are always inclined to that. They're so prosaic," said Harry, getting up. "I must go and see what Van is doing."

He walked away with his usual quick, supple step and casual bearing. They watched his slim figure as he went. Then Romer followed him, slowly.

Vaughan turned to Valentia and said: "I shouldn't if I were you."

"Wouldn't what?"

"Why, meet Harry at half-past three tomorrow morning in the rose garden."

"Good gracious! I never thought of doing such a thing. Besides, it was your idea. . . As a matter of fact, I really assure you it wouldn't be here. It would be in the orchard if anywhere. There is the loveliest cherry-tree there, with a seat all round it."

"How jolly! I'd like to see it. Will you give me the key?"

"Who told you it was kept locked?"

She looked rather annoyed.

"You did, but not intentionally."

"I don't see that you have really any right to suppose—Why shouldn't I go in my own orchard, at any hour I like?"

"But, Val—of course you ought to go in your own orchard. But why don't you meet Romer there?"

"Oh, Gillie, really! . . ."

"He is so straight, so good-looking, and, under all that manner, he's exactly like Vesuvius. Yes. Fancy, you're living with a volcano and you don't appreciate it!"

"Gillie, it's really rather stupid of you to put things like that. It isn't a question of liking either one person *or* another. If Romer were ill, or anything like that, don't you *know*—"

"I know you'd devote yourself to him, like a sister or a mother. You'd put Harry aside for a time as a pleasure that mustn't be indulged in. Now that's just where you're wrong. No! *I* want to see you being ever so good and kind to dear Harry as a duty to a ne'er-do-well of a cousin; and regarding Romer—"

She did not answer.

"My point is," he went on, "that it's really too distressingly conventional of you to suppose that because you happen to be legally married there can be no sort of romance. Only comradeship, or perhaps affectionate sentiment? That's what you believe."

"Isn't it always so?"

"Most often, I grant. That's generally through the man's point of view. But Romer is an exception. He's as much in love as if he had no hope of ever being within a mile of you."

She seemed rather flattered. "Do you really think so? But even that isn't everything."

"Oh, there's a great deal to be done with Romer," was Vaughan's reply.

He spoke with dreamy significance, and she was silent. Then she exclaimed, turning round suddenly—

"I suppose what you really mean is that Harry doesn't care a bit about me?"

"No, I don't. But he cares a bit about a lot of people, and things. He's superficial, and he has no courage."

"No courage? *Harry!*"

"He'd crumble up in a crisis if a strong man took him in hand."

"That's all nonsense." She was growing angry. "Hasn't he been up in an aeroplane, and done—oh, all sorts of things? I call Harry daring and brave!"

"That's all vanity. All that is show and vanity. Oh, Valentia, do forgive me."

"I'll try. . . here he is."

He was seen coming towards them again. Her anger flickered out at once.

"I suppose he thinks we've been here long enough," she said, smiling as women do at such symptoms.

"Of course he does. Vanity—just vanity." Vaughan strolled away.

"Look here! What were you two talking about?"

"Nothing. About you, Harry."

"Rubbish. What was he talking about?"

"You, only you."

"I can't see that that chap's so brilliant! It seems to me he's just like anybody else. And his work shows it too, really. No soul, no real heart in it. All from the outside."

"Nonsense, Harry, nobody is more kind-hearted, more—"

"Look here, Val, I won't have it. Do you hear?"

"Have what, Harry?"

He lowered his voice. "I won't have it. You must go back. It isn't that *I* mind. But Romer will soon think it extraordinary, your sitting out alone so long."

"No, he won't."

"All right then, he won't. He must be an ass," said Harry angrily. "I don't know what he's thinking of. Hasn't he got eyes?"

"Yes, of course he has."

"And eyelids too," said Harry. "I dare say he pretends not to see that Vaughan admires you. Too indolent to bother about it."

"Really. Harry—you go too far. Are you thinking of pointing it out?"

She got up.

"One second," said Harry pleadingly. "It's cruel of you to go now."

"I thought you said we'd better get back?"

"Your hands look so lovely by this light," he spoke in his softest voice.

"We really must go."

"Then at half-past three. I'll bring my sketchbook. Do you know where the key is? Perhaps you've lost it. You are so dreadfully careless." He now spoke in the tone of a reproving husband.

"I've got it. Do you think we'd better? I'm rather tired. Shall you be able to wake?"

Harry turned away.

"All right, it doesn't matter, Val. I shall be going soon, and then—"

She followed him quickly.

"No, no, Harry. Of course."

He gave her a grateful look. They joined the group on the little verandah in front of the house. Van Buren was sitting in the corner and seemed in the depths of depression. From the windows could be heard once more strains of music. Daphne was playing an accompaniment. Muir had again begun the song, and got a little further into it—"*It is not because thy heart is mine, mine only, mine alone.*" But Vaughan came up promptly and stopped it.

XXVII

Seeing the Sun Rise

What a delicate air there was in the garden! There had been a little rain in the night, but Valentia supposed it to be dew. Every little sound seemed the softest music, to the sound of which little dainty things seemed to be dancing in the air. The Green Gate, a red Georgian house, seen in the early glamour with all its blinds down, except one, seemed like a thing half asleep with one eye open.

For a moment she was a little frightened. He was late. She had perhaps got up for nothing. But no, it was worth it. It was lovely here.

Another eye of the house slowly opened, and soon Romeo, or Paolo, or Faust, appeared. True, he was disguised as a flannelled fool, with a sketch-book under his arm. But it *was* Faust, or Romeo, or Paolo, all the same. He looked very handsome. The thought of scoring off other people in the house had raised his spirits and had even made him wake up in time. Valentia's conversation with Vaughan, whom she knew to be honest and believed to be brilliant, had left a certain insidious influence on her which would tell gradually, and yet their talk had had rather a contradictory effect for the moment. She wanted to prove to herself that he was wrong. And Harry felt that his time was growing short. Very soon he must put an end to it all.

This thought made him more affectionate. It occurred to him for a moment that he would tell her in the orchard; but, of course, he didn't. Every day he thought he would tell her, and something always happened to prevent it. Besides, there would have to be a quarrel anyhow at the end, so why make it longer than necessary?

They sat down under the cherry-tree.

"Fancy you, Valentia, a minion of the moon, rising before dawn! Let me look at you. You fill me with wonder and joy."

"Did you mind getting up *very* much, Harry?"

"It *was* rather hard. Listen! . . . That's a thrush, making a scene with another thrush in the tree."

"Is it? How do you know?"

"Of course it is! How do *you* know things? How did you know exactly what to wear, Val? I knew you had clothes for every possible occasion; but still, to choose the *exact* right dress to put on to meet your cousin at dawn in the orchard seems—well, rather extraordinary. Pinkish blue—or is it bluish pink?—to match the sky. How jolly! It fastens in front."

"Well, of course I couldn't expect Ogburn to get up in the middle of the night."

"And no hatpins for once, thank goodness."

"Well, if we *sat up* till now I shouldn't be wearing a hat, should I?"

"Don't argue. It's too early."

"It isn't really early. It's very late."

"Oh, Val! You're being logical."

He took her hands and looked at them, and quoted—

> *"They are pale with the pallor of ivories,*
> *But they blush at the tips like a curved sea-shell."*

"Oh, Harry!"

He was thinking. He looked almost miserable. "I don't see—I must admit—how I shall ever be able to leave your hands!"

She looked at him suspiciously.

"Why should you? What do you mean?"

"Nothing. I only meant I couldn't. . ."

"Oh!"

"What's that? . . . Some one coming along the lawn."

"Doesn't it sound curious?" she said—"so *rustly*!"

"Who can it be? Surely your friend Vaughan couldn't get up at this hour."

"Nonsense! Of course not. They're coming here." She jumped up.

"Go and open the gate at once," said Harry, giving her the key. "I'll wait here a minute." While she obeyed he used a good deal of language. He now felt that he would give all he possessed to keep her there five minutes longer.

"Fancy! It's Romer!" exclaimed Valentia. "He hasn't seen me yet."

"Go to him at *once*. Tell him you got up to see the sun rise. I'll come directly and join you. Oh, confound it! *Do* look sharp. Seem pleased to see him." He spoke in a harsh tone of command.

She ran to meet Romer, saying jokingly, "Fancy meeting you!"

"I thought you'd be here. I went to your room and found you were out. Thought I'd get up early."

"I'm so glad. *Isn't* it lovely and worth seeing here? Come and pick some fruit in the orchard."

"No, thanks."

"Oh, *do*! Harry's devouring gooseberries. He's sketching the sky."

"Why doesn't Harry come?" said Romer.

He had no expression, and it was always impossible to guess by his looks or his tone what he was thinking or feeling, except when he smiled.

"Here he is."

Harry joined them.

"Good gracious, old boy! Who in the world—! What on earth made you come out so early?"

Romer now smiled and looked at Valentia admiringly.

"Gardener's not up yet. Thought perhaps I'd mow the lawn," he said apologetically.

XXVIII

"Reply Paid"

Valentia had been hurt at the tone in which Harry had given his orders, and turned from him to help to find the mowing-machine.

"Doesn't she look jolly at sunrise? All that pink and mauve in the sky tones in so well. It seems to suit her. That's how she really should be painted," said Harry, in the tone of an artist admiring his model. "Don't you think so?"

"Yes," said Romer.

"She looks like a golden rose," Harry went on. He wanted to please Val, who he saw was annoyed with him, and to emphasise the openness of his admiration to Romer. "Doesn't she?"

"Quite," said her husband.

Harry felt the morning was spoilt and the situation absurd. He could not bear to be thwarted in any way. He went back to his own room, bounced angrily on to his bed, and went to sleep again, after having seen Valentia through the window helping to push the mower, and saying to himself—

"How like a woman! I shall go up to town with Van Buren and send a wire to Alec."

This was his revenge.

Their momentary fears about Romer were completely dissipated. He seemed exactly as usual. As a rule he was even-tempered. Not many people had seen him put out, though he could be very angry, except with Valentia. During this day he seemed, for him, a little irritable. Perhaps, Val thought, through getting up too early.

Harry went up to town with Van Buren for the day, intending to return the same evening. He soon recovered himself in the course of copious confidences in the train. As soon as he had arrived in London he began to count the minutes before he should go back.

Valentia expected the elder Mrs. Wyburn to lunch.

"What shall we do with her today?" Val asked Daphne. "She must be kept in a good temper, because it's the last time she'll come down before going to Bournemouth. It's rather a pity they've all gone. Romer is sure to say the wrong thing to her—let out some trifle that we have been carefully concealing for months—praise up Harry, or something."

"Doesn't she like Harry?"

"Since he went to see her she likes him for herself, but not for me."

"What cheek! But he's not here."

"No, if he were she might like him again all right. Then, Romer talks too slowly for her. Her mind works quicker than his, and one can only deal with him by racing on in front, and turning round to beckon. With Mrs. Wyburn there are only two things that are any use—dash and volubility. It's difficult to keep the thing going when she's alone with us."

"Well, why not pass the time this afternoon by returning the Campbells' visit, and take Mrs. Wyburn with us to 'The Angles'?" Daphne suggested.

"Oh no! It's treating them almost like royalty to go so soon. And there's the Belgian man."

"Doesn't she like Belgians then, Val?"

"I've never asked her. Only, don't you see, it isn't that but the Belgian is what Harry calls a blighter—a beano-blighter; and so is Mrs. Wyburn, and it doesn't do to have two beano-blighters in the same party."

"Ah, I see; they'd clash. What *is* a beano-blighter exactly, Val?"

"A person who blights beanos. Who makes every one a little uncomfortable, casts a gloom over entertainments—has to be taken in hand and dealt with separately from the others—doesn't blend, you know."

"You mean some one who isn't the life and soul of the party?"

"No, I don't. That's almost as bad in its way. In fact, the life-and-soul-of-the-party person casts almost as great a gloom on the rest as a blighter."

"Oh dear! Yes, I see."

"We must meet her at the station in the motor. I shall put on my blue serge and my plain sailor. She mustn't see me in the garden without a hat, nor in a real one. You do the same, Daphne."

"But my sailor's too large in the head, and that makes it fall over my eyes, and that gives it a Frenchy look, like *L'Art et la Mode*," protested Daphne.

"Stuff it with paper. Here's the *Bystander*."

"Oh, isn't it a pity? There's such a pretty picture of—"

"Oh, don't bother."

Mrs. Wyburn was gracious today, and all was going well when, about half-past five, a telegram, reply paid, was brought. It was addressed to Harry.

"What shall we do?"

"Why, keep it till he comes. He'll be back to dinner," Romer said.

"Suppose it's something urgent," said Val, seeming a little agitated. "Don't you think perhaps we ought to open it? He won't mind."

"You can't. It's addressed to Harry," said Romer.

Mrs. Wyburn's quick eyes took in some signs of tension, but she continued giving them advice about the garden. She thought the flowers too florid, and was always a little shocked at the extravagant scent and exuberance of the roses. She seemed to think they should be kept more in their place—not allowed to climb all over the house, and romp or lean about the garden doing just what they liked. She had winced in the drawing-room, relented in the dining-room, and refrained, really, only in the kitchen, that she had insisted upon seeing. It was the only room to the decoration of which she gave whole-hearted praise and approval. The cooking at the Green Gate she admitted to be perfect, without pretension. In fact, she thought everything in the house a little overdone, except the mutton.

"I can't think who that wire can be from," Val said several times to Daphne when her mother-in-law had gone. She meant that she could think.

"Well, you'll know directly. Harry's arriving."

Harry found it in the hall, and came in with it.

"You open it for me," he said, giving it to Val.

Since his last instructions to Alec he felt perfectly safe.

She read—

Thousand thanks awfully bucked at letter at Queens' Hotel Cowes for three days could you join us there wire reply fondest love and kisses.

Johnson

XXIX

Gladys

On arriving in London, Vaughan found his secretary with the usual heaps of letters. One envelope, addressed in a large and rather infantine hand, was put aside for him. The note ran—

The Baldfaced Stag,
Edgware

Dear Mr. Vaughan,

"I eard only yesterday that the play you kindly sent me and mother to was wrote by you, I call it a shame you didn't tell me before, we saw the name on the programme, but never thought it could be the same but yesterday mother saw a piece in the paper about you in the weekly dispatch and she said it was the same, I'm sory I said the people in the play went on silly I beg pardon for calling the play silly I wouldnt have done it if Id known, so hope youre not angry, they seemed to me to go on silly, but I dont reelly know much about those kind of ladies and gentlemen, we saw the piece in the paper only yesterday and mother said it was the same, we hope you will soon come again to tea the calf is better believe me yours truly

GLADIS ADELAIDE BRILL

He instantly wrote back—

Dear Miss Brill,

"I am *so* relieved and thankful to hear the calf is better, all the more because I had no idea it had been indisposed. I fancied, though, it was looking a little pale the last time I had the pleasure of meeting it in the field. Please don't think again of your criticism. It gave me very great pleasure. You must think me very foolish. You could say nothing that I would not like except to ask me not to come and see you. I am very busy just now and so have little time for afternoon calls, but will come one of these days soon.

Yours always,
GILBERT HEREFORD VAUGHAN

He waited a moment, and then added—

"I will turn up tomorrow at four. Try not to forget me till then."

For the rest of the day he was in high spirits. The letter seemed to keep him up through the various little bothers of the day. He had been going to France for the summer. He admitted to himself that this semi-flirtation was keeping him in England. He didn't like the idea of going away very long from the possibility of turning up at the "Bald-faced Stag."

The explanation Harry gave about Johnson's telegram satisfied Valentia for the time, as he declined the invitation to Cowes, but the incident left an uneasy feeling in Val's mind. She could not bear to own to herself that he was deceiving her, and he hadn't the courage to give it away yet, not that he cared so very much about hurting her, but he was happier at the Green Gate than anywhere else. He liked the house, the atmosphere, and Romer; but what kept him most was, of course, that curious charm Valentia had for him, which was perhaps stronger than ever because he knew that the end was not far off. He often thought he was a fool not to have taken the opportunity to break it off on this occasion. He couldn't stand the idea of not seeing her, just because of the way her hair grew on her forehead! So low, and in such thick waves! Alec Walmer's hair, also fair, was thin and unmeaning. She had a low forehead, and yet the hair began high up. In the evening when it was carefully arranged, and the iron had entered into it, it looked like a stiff transformation, even worse than when left to nature.

But of course, in spite of the reconciliation, a residue of mistrust remained, and on his side a sensation of restlessness which left him irritable; less amiable and pleasant than usual.

They were sitting on the little terrace. He was smoking and reading the paper. He suddenly threw it down and said—

"How quiet you are, Val! Why don't you talk?"

"I don't think I've got anything to say."

"You seem depressed," he said, rather aggressively.

"I feel a little depressed."

Harry gave expression to the usual injustice of the unfaithful.

"What a mistake women make in being gloomy! How foolish it is. Shall I tell you the key of the whole situation between men and women?"

"Do."

"Well, dear, it's just—a *smile*. Never be dull, never be ill, never be depressed. Be gay—always gay. That's what men like—that's the one thing that they go out for and come in for—a smile."

"Your ideal of a woman seems to be a Cheshire cat," she answered, looking rather amused. "Your motto is, like the man in *The Arcadians*: Always Merry and Bright. Well, I'm sure there's a good deal in it. But I'm not usually accused of being a dreary person."

"Of course you're not; you're charming, lively, amusing, sympathetic. That's your great attraction, Val. But the last few days you seem rather to have lost it."

"You can hardly resent my feeling a little down, Harry. One or two little things that have happened lately have made me anxious."

"Never be anxious. You ought to trust, trust—always trust."

"Oh, that's all very well! That wire. . ."

"Are we going to have that all over again? I thought I'd explained." He assumed the air of a patient martyr.

"I know you *explained* all right. Well, I won't think about it any more. Don't be horrid, Harry. . . Have you seen this week's *Punch*? There's something in it simply *too* heavenly—such a joke! Let me read it to you."

"It's very sweet of you—but do you ever realise—I wonder if it's ever struck you, Val, that men aren't always in the mood for heavenly jokes? There are times when one likes to think—to see life as it is—to discuss abstract things, even."

"Oh! Well. . . what do you think of Daphne's dress? Isn't it pretty? It was made by Ogburn, all out of nothing, in no time."

He looked at Daphne, who was sitting under a tree reading Cyril's last letter over again.

"It's all right. It suits *her*. I don't call *that* a serious subject."

"What subject would you like, then?"

"Well—Romer, for instance. Where is he?"

"Talking to the gardener about mowing. Do you want him? I'll call him if you like."

"Dear Val, it's not quite like you to be ironical to *me* . . . You ought not to laugh at Romer either. I'm complex, perhaps—I know I am; but it jars on me when you do that."

She stared at him.

"Look here—I know I'm tiresome," said Harry, returning to his usual caressing manner. "Don't take any notice of it. It's—the weather, I think, or want of exercise. I'll go and improvise a little."

He pushed back his chair, and, with a parting look of forgiveness, he went into the house and began to improvise (rather dismally) a well-known funeral march. Or perhaps it was only a coincidence. Perhaps he would have thought of it if Chopin hadn't.

Harry was only musical by fits and starts, and generally either to impress some one or because he was out of temper. Val never regarded it as a good sign when he grappled with the Steinway.

In ten minutes he had grown tired of his mood of melody, and strolled into the rose garden with a book.

Yes, certainly Harry was restless.

XXX

The Angles

"You're very quiet, Val," remarked Daphne, as they flew along in the motor on their way to call on the Prebendary's wife at The Angles.

Both sisters wore little cottage bonnets, blue motor-veils, and large loose white coats with high collars.

"How can I talk when we're exceeding the speed limit?" said Valentia.

"You usually do. Is anything the matter?"

"No, nothing at all... Harry's been horrid lately."

"I suppose he *is* occasionally."

"No, he's not. He's got the artistic temperament, and of course he can't always be the same, poor dear."

"What a pity one can't be an artist without having the artistic temperament! It always seems to mean being late for meals, and losing your temper, or being amusing when every one wants to go to bed."

"As a matter of fact," said Valentia, "I never knew any one with less of it than Harry. There isn't a more hard-headed business man in the world in his way, though he *has* read poetry and plays the piano sometimes, and paints. He is an artist too... but—well, not in any of the recognised arts... I hear Miss Luscombe and Rathbone—I mean Mr. and Mrs. Rathbone—have gone to Oberammergau for their honeymoon."

"Oh! Is that the latest thing to do?"

"Of course not, Daphne, but she thinks it is. Miss Luscombe has spent her life in trying to catch the last omnibus and always just missing it, and she's not going to leave off now just because she happens to be married. Here we are!"

The Prebendary's wife received them very graciously. Her waist looked longer than ever, and her skirt seemed more than usually abnormal in width. She did all that she could to entertain them. She showed them her son Garstin's map of Buckinghamshire, and then said—

"I'll send for Mr. Stoendyck. He's upstairs inventing. You can't *think* how clever he is and how hard he works. It's really wonderful! We often leave him alone for hours to think things out, and sometimes he plays sonatas; he says it refreshes him. He really is an extraordinary man."

Mr. Stoendyck came in, looking very martial and scientific and pleased with himself, as though he had just invented gunpowder. Mrs. Campbell began as usual to talk baby language, and play a kind of Dumb Crambo at him. He never seemed able to guess the word.

"I hope we haven't interrupted you in your studies," said Val politely.

"She say she ope she not interrupt. Work, you know. Oeuvre—Arbeit."

"I was just amusing myself with the very witty paper from Germany, *Kladderadatsch*. It is very funny," he said.

"It sounds funny," said Val sympathetically.

"What I find in England is that you're all wonderfully serious, wonderfully courteous, wonderfully kind"—he bowed to his hostess; "but, you'll excuse my saying so, I don't find enough wit or lightness for my temperament. For humour I have to go to Belgium or Germany."

He spoke with intense solemnity.

Mrs. Campbell now began to translate him even to himself.

"You say you like fun, wit—just fun to make laugh?" She made strange signs with her fingers.

He did not appear to understand the code. He stared at her with a frown, and rasped on seriously—

"I find a few comical jokes occasionally a great relief after my heavy work. It is very deep work."

"I suppose it would be indiscreet to ask what the invention is?" said Valentia, smiling.

"Not at all. There is nothing indiscreet whatever in your curiosity, Mrs. Wyburn."

He took a scone covered with butter and swallowed it in an extraordinarily short time, and in an ingenious manner.

"No, there's no indiscretion in the matter at all. Do not trouble yourself on that score. It is merely the natural interest that a cultivated and intellectual English lady would naturally take when she hears of an extraordinary invention from another country." He bowed, and having thus explained her to herself, he then ate another scone.

"She say she want to know, you know," nodded Mrs. Campbell, putting up a playful and threatening finger with dignified coquetry and a stony smile. (She was subject to fits of this kind of marble archness unexpectedly.)

"Yes. So I understood."

The Belgian was looking at Daphne with distinct admiration. Of course Miss Campbell came and sat down beside him. Women always follow their instinct to come and sit on the other side of any man whom they regard as their property. They seem to think that merely by sitting on the other side they protect him from freebooters. As a matter of fact, it would be more sensible, if to distract his attention were the object, to sit opposite with some one else.

Mr. Stoendyck turned his back on her completely, and said to Daphne—

"Very charming, those motor-veils, and the whole costume. At the same time, while being thoroughly practical and sensible, it is, if I may say so, extremely becoming."

He bowed with a condescending air, and went on—

"The English young girl—at least, such specimens as I have seen in the neighbourhood, especially in the country—seems to me a wonderfully beautiful object. In Belgium we are getting on, but we have not reached, as yet, the point of freedom combined with modesty that you constantly see over here. Particularly, as I say, in rural districts."

He then made what can only be described, vulgarly, as a distinct 'eye.'

Both the Campbells looked uneasy.

"The Prebendary will be in soon," said Mrs. Campbell. "He promised faithfully to come back to tea today. He also is a very busy man. He come in soon," she spoke reassuringly.

Daphne was suddenly taken with a *fou rire* and began to laugh helplessly. Val, seeing her condition, and knowing that when she once started there was no hope but in immediate flight, took leave.

They were cordially asked to come again by Mrs. Campbell. But Mr. Stoendyck invited them to lunch, and wanted to fix a day and hour. Mrs. Campbell, however, declined his invitation for them. Mrs. Wyburn, she said, must have a great many engagements.

They left Stoendyck standing in the hall, looking sentimental.

"All foreigners not of the Latin race go on like that," said Val, as they drove back. "They may be scientific, or soldiers, philosophers, or musicians, but if they're Germans or Belgians or Austrians, or anything of that sort, they always get bowled over by a young girl, a blue ribbon, plumpness, or fair hair."

"But I'm very thin and dark," said Daphne angrily.

"I don't care if you are. You're a pretty girl, you're unmarried, you've got blue chiffon round your head—and there it is. . . I don't mean Prussian officers, of course."

"*They* would appreciate *you*, I suppose you mean!"

"One can't say. They'd probably take on anything."

Valentia took out the little looking-glass from her motor-bag, looked at it, put it back, and added—

"Anything possible, I mean."

"Go on, Val."

"Go on how?"

"Telling me things. You're so interesting, you know such a lot. Now, about the Latin races—wouldn't they like—er—me?"

"Of course they would. But they'd like you better if you were married to Cyril or any one. Frenchmen and Italians always want their love-making or flirtations to have something in it of the nature of a *score*. They love scoring off a third person, whoever it may be,—whether it's their friend's wife, or their wife's friend, or anything."

"They're not sincere, then?"

"Don't be silly. If they weren't sincere, why are there nothing but unwritten-law crimes all over France and Italy? And why do Parisians think and talk of. . . nothing else! They're *sincere* all right: it's their hobby. Italians, of course, are more jealous and faithful, and Parisians are frightfully vain—there's a good deal of a sort of snobbism about it. They love to show off. That's why they're so keen on dress."

"Do you think," said Daphne, with sudden anxiety, "that if you don't dress to perfection you can't keep a man's love? I *do* hope not! I mean because when I'm married to Cyril I shan't be able to afford to wear anything at all, except a clean blouse which I shall have to iron out myself, like in *Hearth and Home*."

Valentia shook her head.

"Dressing to perfection doesn't make men love you, silly. It only makes women hate you. And I never have yet seen the advantage of that."

"Oh, then, do Parisians want other women to hate you?" asked Daphne. Her sister hesitated.

"Sometimes. Very often they don't. They want you to be admired by other people, whoever they are, men or women. But in Paris dress counts in a different sort of way—it means more—it stands for more. Oh, don't bother!"

"Well, give me a straightforward Englishman!" exclaimed Daphne.

"Yes, indeed!" replied Val. "That Belgian Herr, anyhow, doesn't count. I can't think why Mrs. Preb. and Miss Campbell are so much in love with him."

"Isn't it funny? Why do you think it is, Val?"

"Perhaps it's because he's a man. You see, they're accustomed to curates."

XXXI

At Edgware

M iss Brill had twisted up her hair and put on her Sunday dress to receive Vaughan.

To harmonise with the Dickens's garden it ought to have been white muslin with flounces and a pink sash. But it was a quite long, dark blue Liberty satin, made by a smart dressmaker in the Finchley Road. It had a high collar, an Empire waist, and gathers.

Her mother was delighted with it. Gladys had not been quite satisfied herself, and had tried to tie it in round the ankles with concealed string, to make it look more like a nobble skirt, as she called it.

Her almost too abundant hair had been piled over a pad, which gave her the appearance of having a swollen head. Yet even so she looked lovely, rather like an old-fashioned picture in the Academy of *I'se Gan'ma*, or something of the kind, suggesting a baby disguised as a grown-up-person.

Vaughan went through the usual ritual of asking after Mrs. Brill— he rather hurried Mr. Brill over his remark about the finest woman one would see in a day's march—then admired the weather, ordered tea, and asked for Miss Brill.

Gladys came and sat down with a rather shy, self-conscious air.

She soon lost it, however, and began to get natural again.

"Oh, Mr. Vaughan! I *never* was more surprised than I was at that piece in the paper! And mother come over quite queer, she was so surprised. You were kind in your letter to forgive me for being rude. Who'd ever have thought you was clever?"

"Who, indeed! But, Gladys, why this get-up? Why are you dressed up in satin and dark colours on a summer day?"

"Why, mother said a nice navy blue was always useful. I'd rather have had a Cambridge blue myself. Mother says navy blue's so ladylike. Don't you like it?"

"Charming. But I don't like what you've done to your hair."

"Don't you, though? Fancy! Well, I don't seem to care much for it myself. It's a Pompadour, you know—a pad."

"Take it off," said Vaughan.

"Oh, I can't!"

"All right, *I* will. Come in the field."

"Well, I don't mind if you do. I'll say I took my hair down because it was heavy."

"You've tried to spoil yourself, but you haven't succeeded. Why did you do it, Gladys?"

"Seeing you was clever, I thought pr'aps I'd better try to look more grown-up."

"Ah! what a mistake! Your great charm is that you're such a regular J.F."

"What's that?"

"A *jeune fille.*"

"What does that mean? What's a J.F. in English?"

"A jolly flapper."

"Oh, I say!"

In the field Vaughan, with several interruptions and reproaches for being a caution, managed to take the pad off her head and to throw it in the field. But an unfortunate thing happened. All the corn-coloured hair fell down over his face and he had kissed her—by accident—before he knew it.

"Oh, I say! You are a caution!" was her only remark. But she did not laugh, and as she hastily did a little amateur coiffing, he thought she looked slightly annoyed. At any rate, she hadn't much more to say to him, and he went back to London almost immediately, feeling quite absurdly agitated about such an unimportant trifle.

An hour later, when quietly at home in his study, Vaughan was suddenly seized by that species of madness that has been known to wreck careers, "to launch a thousand ships," to cause all kinds of chaos. It was that terrible *once-on-board-the-lugger-and-the-girl-is-mine-I-must-and-shall-possess-her* feeling in its most acute form. Most men have known it at some time in their lives. He thought of Harry de Freyne, and felt noble and superior in contrast to what *his* conduct would have been, as he sat down and wrote with intense pleasure—

Darling Gladys,
"I love you. Will you marry me? Please try. I'm writing to your father. Don't keep me waiting long for the answer.
Yours for always,
Gillie

He then wrote a long and sensible letter to Mr. Brill; all business, respect, and urgency, saying he knew that Gladys was very young, but that he would make her happy, and so forth.

These two letters he sent off by express messenger in a taxicab to the "Bald-faced Stag," and then sat down to dinner.

What a dinner! And what an evening he spent! He planned a long journey—what fun to show the child new places and things! Why shouldn't he marry the charming, refined, and beautiful daughter of an hotel-keeper? He decided even on alterations in the house, and he meant to be ecstatically happy.

What did he care for people? He had never lived either to *épater* the *bourgeois* or to satisfy the ideal of the gentleman next door. He was going to do something *he* liked! . . .

He woke up the next morning at six o'clock with a ghastly chilly horror on him. What had he done? Had he been mad? To marry Miss Brill, the daughter of the landlord of a little suburban public-house! A girl of sixteen, pretty enough certainly, but with no pretensions to being a lady, no possibility of having anything in common with him. But it wasn't so much the question of what people would say—of course, most of the women he knew would drop him, and the men would laugh at him and make love to her—but, how long would it last? How long would this strange mania endure? Perhaps not a week. The poor child would have an awful time, too. She was much happier as she was.

Well! He was a sportsman, and had taken the risk. He must wait now. At the back of his mind he was wondering how he could get out of it.

He had not to wait long. His letters were answered by the first post. Evidently, the "Bald-faced Stag" had been kept up late that night to reply in time.

Gladys wrote very respectfully that she was very sorry she hadn't told him before, but she was privately engaged to the son of the landlord of the Green Man at Stanmore: the Eldest Son, she wrote with pride (as though he would inherit the title). She was awfully sorry. Besides, she was going to be a manicure, first, for two years, and then settle down at Stanmore. Her fiancé was twenty-one. She hoped Mr. Vaughan would come over to tea very soon, and she thought his letter was very kind, and remained his truly, Gladys Brill.

Mr. Brill had written a long and slightly rambling letter which suggested rough copies and even some assistance from the old vintages of the "Bald-faced Stag." He refused most firmly, though thoroughly sensible of the honour done him by Mr. Vaughan's offer, but he couldn't go back on his word to his friend at the Green Man. The arrangement had been made, when Gladys and the son were in their cradles, by him and his pal of the Green Man and he couldn't go back on his word. And Gladys liked the young chap; and it was a great honour, indeed, that Mr. Vaughan had done them, and it would have been splendid for Gladys in the worldly sense. But there! it was better, perhaps, not to mix up Stations. Mr. Brill repeated this sentiment over and over again, always using a capital S for station—(as though Vaughan had expressed an insane desire to confuse Victoria with the Great Western). And he remained very respectfully, Tom Brill.

"A manicure in Bond Street and then the landlady of a common country inn! Never! She shan't! I'll go down and persuade her. I'll make them come round."

Vaughan was so hurt and disappointed that he felt he could never smile again.

But he did.

XXXII

Tension

When the sisters came back from their drive Harry was sitting on the little marble terrace reading *Count Florio and Phillis K.* and smoking cigarettes. With almost conjugal unfairness he complained that Valentia always went out just before he arrived. In fact, he had begged her to get the visit over that afternoon, as he intended to be late.

Valentia sat down and began a lively account of "The Angles," but he implored her not to describe those awful people at home, and particularly not to tell him anything about that poisonous Belgian. Then he told Val that blue didn't suit her, and, when she agreed with him, petulantly complained that she had no ideas of her own.

"But I had an idea of my own; only now you say it's wrong."

"So it is. But, even if it is wrong, you should stick to it. You should have more individuality."

"What an awful word," she said.

"What's the matter with the word?"

"Nothing. It's so long."

"You're talking nonsense, Valentia."

"Well, why shouldn't I talk nonsense? I'm sure I've heard you say there's nothing so depressing as a woman with no nonsense about her."

"I know. But there needn't be nothing else."

"Harry, are you trying to quarrel? If so I'd better go away."

"Oh, all right! Very well! Do as you like," said Harry. "It seems a curious way to treat a guest: to go out when you expect him, and then the moment you come in to make an excuse to leave him alone again. But please yourself!"

He took up his book and turned away.

Valentia went into the house, to her room, and sat down opposite the looking-glass with a sigh. It was at moments like these that she sometimes thought, with a slight reaction, of Romer. Romer was never capricious, never irritable, never trying. It was true that he rarely answered her except in monosyllables, but yet she knew that he delighted in and tacitly encouraged her fluency. He did not respond to every idea she expressed as Harry did (when Harry was in a good temper), but she knew she had no better audience. His extreme quietness might be admitted, occasionally, to cast a slight gloom, but negatively what enormous advantages his silence had! Romer never scolded, never laid down the law; never thought it necessary to give her long, minute, detailed accounts of his impressions of art, or life, or literature; never insisted on pointing out, as if it were a matter of life and death, precisely where he differed in his opinions of a book, a play, or an incident, from the criticisms in the daily papers. Nor did he refer to some annoying past incident half a dozen times a day as a sealed subject. He had other qualities. He could take tickets, he could sign cheques (and even seemed to like doing it). He could see about things. He wasn't selfish. Yes, Valentia thought, when she saw Harry at his worst, that perhaps she didn't really quite appreciate her husband. How irritating Harry would have been in that capacity!

Daphne came in, and Valentia went on, as usual, with her thoughts aloud.

"Wouldn't Harry be a maddening husband?" she said as she brushed out her hair.

"Oh! Would he? In what way?"

"He'd be so selfish, so obtrusive—he'd always want you to do exactly what he liked, just when he liked, and never when he didn't, or when you liked, I mean."

"How could he like you to do what he liked when he didn't like? That would be expecting too much. I don't see what you mean, Val."

"I only mean that when he's in a bad temper Harry's tiresome, and if he were married he'd be in one oftener."

"Oh dear! Are most men bad-tempered when they're married, Val?"

"Yes. Nearly always."

"*What?* Then, will Cyril. . ."

"Cyril's a pleasant, easy-going boy, but, as you won't have enough money, he's sure to be bad-tempered at times."

"Then aren't married men bad-tempered when they have plenty of money, Val?"

"Oh, if they have a great deal they're awfully bad-tempered, too; because, you see, then they lose it, or if they don't do that they're always trying to enjoy themselves with it and finding the enjoyment flat, and then they blame their wives. Besides, anyhow, having enough money leads to all sorts of complications."

"Oh dear! Then what do you advise?" Daphne hung on Valentia's words, respecting her superior knowledge and experience.

"Oh, I advise enough, anyhow. It can't make you happy, but it can avoid certain troubles. Love in a cottage is only all right for the week-end when you have a nice house in London as well, and a season ticket or a motor, and electric light and things, and a telephone. Oh, by the way, our telephone here is eating its head off. We never use it. Go and ring up to the grocer, not to forget to send the things, will you, dear? He's got a telephone, too—the only tradesman in the village who has."

"What things isn't he to forget to send?"

"How should I know?—the usual things. He never does forget, but it looks well to remind him, and the 'phone needs exercise."

"All right. But before I go, Val—suppose you can't have the sort of love-in-a-cottage you mean, and there's no fear of your being so rich that it makes you miserable, what is the best thing to do?"

"Why, I suppose the old business in the old novels, a competence with the man of your heart, would do all right."

Daphne looked pleased.

"For six months, anyhow. Or a year or two, perhaps," Val added.

"Oh dear!" cried Daphne again, as she left the room.

"Poor pet," Val murmured to herself. "I hope I'm not teaching her to be cynical."

XXXIII

Good-bye

The only person in the family who did not thoroughly approve of Gladys's decision was her mother. Mrs. Brill thought it sheer madness to decline proposals of a 'gentleman from the West End,' as she called him; so clever and so rich, so handsome and so much in love. She was romantic and yet worldly in her views, and was much excited at the idea of the rivalry for her daughter. There were bitter scenes between Mr. and Mrs. Brill on the subject. Mr. Brill was not romantic nor worldly, but he was very sentimental, and he didn't hold with breaking his word to the Green Man, nor indeed with that mixing up of Stations to which he had already alluded.

Between the opposing views of her parents Gladys became somewhat bewildered. She liked the son of the Green Man (he was in reality only a green boy, but good-looking, and she had always known him), and she wished to be loyal to him. Yet her mother's remarks about Mr. Vaughan began to appeal to her imagination, such as it was. She was rather dazzled and began to weaken. She was at the age when one can really be in love with anybody, and she was flattered. Though she felt she would feel more at home with her childhood's friend, she began, very slightly, to look down upon him when she compared him with Gillie.

Vaughan came down the day after he had received her letter, and behaved precisely as usual.

Mr. Brill, meeting him with a rather shamefaced air in the garden, said straightforwardly—

"Very pleased indeed to see you, Mr. Vaughan. You got my letter, sir?"

"Yes, indeed. To my sorrow. I want to talk to you about it."

"Well, I was sorry to write it, sir, if you take my meaning. But there! Well, Mrs. Brill 'as expressed a wish for a few words with you, if you wouldn't mind."

"I shall be delighted, of course. But—may I see Gladys?"

"Why, yes, sir. Tea and bread and butter? The usual thing?"

"Yes, please. As usual." Mr. Brill lingered.

"Ave some watercress with it, sir," he added sympathetically, "or we've got some very nice little radishes. Ow about them?"

Vaughan nearly laughed.

"No, thank you! I'm afraid they wouldn't be any use to me, Mr. Brill."

"Ha, ha! You will have your joke!"

Mr. Brill went in and told his wife that Mr. Vaughan was "sitting there looking that miserable it was enough to make one's heart ache."

With this satisfactory intelligence he sent Gladys into the garden.

She was all blushes and shyness. Her hair had gone back into the long plait, and she wore her schoolgirl dress again.

"You're too proud, Gladys!" he said reproachfully. "Why did you never tell me of your engagement?"

"Why, I didn't ardly count it to interest you, Mr. Vaughan. Besides, it's not to be for two years."

"Are you in love with him?"

"Why, what a question! I *like* him. He's a nice boy."

"I suppose he's very much in love with you?"

"Oh, he's all right."

"That was a very cruel letter you wrote me, Gladys."

"I was afraid you'd think it rude," she answered apologetically.

"No, dear. It isn't rude to refuse a proposal. You can't accept them all, can you?"

"You've made a wretched tea, Mr. Vaughan. Is there anything else you'd like?"

"Yes, I want to go in the field again, like the day before yesterday."

"Was it only the day before yesterday? So it was. A lot seems to ave appened since. Well, come along."

She looked such an absolute child as she climbed the gate that Gillie felt almost ashamed of his proposal, and thought that probably her father was quite right. . . But her face was so exactly like Sir Joshua Reynolds' angels' heads, she might have sat for them. She was too absurdly pretty. And sweet, too, he thought. She had no vulgar pretensions, she was simple. She only wanted a little polish. He could teach her everything necessary. No task could have been more congenial. . .

"So you think I'm too old for you. Is that it?"

"No, it isn't. It isn't that. It's what father told you."

"Would you hate to go for a long journey with me, to see other places, other countries?"

"Oh no; I'd like it. We went to Clacton last summer. It *was* fun."

He thought a little.

"Gladys, as you're so young, won't you leave the whole thing in abeyance for a time?"

"In what, did you say?"

"Undecided. Let me come and talk to you about it in six months. The only thing I can't bear you to do is to be a manicure. I'm going to speak to your mother about it. I can't stand it."

"Oh, why, Mr. Vaughan? I should have thought it was nice for me to sort of better myself."

"Nonsense. Far better stay here. Well, will you agree to that?"

"To give up the manicuring and to leave the engagement open like? Is that what you mean?"

"That's the idea."

She thought a minute.

"I really don't see how I can. And—my boy would feel it something cruel if I put him off like that."

"When do you see him?" he asked jealously.

"Why, on Sundays. Only on Sundays."

"Ah, that's why I've never seen him. I wondered why I'd never met my hated rival."

She laughed.

"Oh, now, you're going on silly, like the people in the play! . . . I don't believe you alf mean it."

"Don't you believe I love you?"

"How can you? You don't ardly know me, except as a friend."

"I'll tell you why I love you if you like, dearest."

"Well, why?" She spoke with girlish curiosity.

"Because you're lovely, and lovable, and sweet. Because you're a darling."

"Oh, I say!"

"Doesn't your boy, as you call him, say these things to you?"

"Not like that. I only see him on Sundays."

"And does he kiss you on Sundays?"

"Oh yes."

Vaughan got up.

"All right, I won't worry you any more. . . I'll let you be happy in your own way, dear. . . I must go now."

"Oh, *must* you?"

She seemed very disappointed.

"Yes, I'm going to France."

"What, today?"

"No, next week."

"Oh, I am sorry."

"Good-bye, dear."

He went in and bid adieu to Mr. and Mrs. Brill and the "Bald-faced Stag" for ever. He said to her father that he was resigned.

As soon as he had gone, Gladys went upstairs to her room, looked in the glass, then burst out crying.

She had fallen in love with Gillie.

XXXIV

ROMER OVERHEARS

Romer started to go by himself for a five-mile walk, leaving Daphne, Valentia and Harry in the garden, but a nail in his boot hurt so much that, after the first half-mile, Romer decided he couldn't stand it any longer, and would walk back, go quietly in, and then surprise them by coming to tea in the garden.

He was gone a very short time, but he hastened his steps, looking forward immensely to the removal of the boot, and also to seeing Valentia again.

Lately he had been more than ever devoted to her. Ever since they had been at the Green Gate she had been specially gentle and charming—but not nearly so lively as usual. Sometimes she looked quite anxious and preoccupied. He thought, too, that she was occasionally irritable; which was unlike her—and her spirits varied continually.

He asked her one day what was the matter, and she assured him that there was nothing, so he believed her. But he was always thinking about her, trying to find some means to please her. He was dissatisfied about her.

He came back, went into his room, and his spirits incalculably raised by the cessation of the torture, he went and sat by the window, and looked out at the lovely garden.

It was a hot summer day; a little wind was in the trees.

Exactly under the window, on the little verandah, sat Harry with Valentia. Daphne was no longer there.

They were talking; and talking, it seemed to him, in an agitated way.

Leaning a little over he could see Valentia on a bamboo chair. To his horror he saw that she was crying.

Harry, speaking in a suppressed but rather angry voice, appeared to be trying to comfort her.

Without a second's hesitation or a moment's scruple, Romer intently listened. He did not hide or draw behind the curtain. He remained in full view, in the window, so that they could see him easily if they happened to look up. But they did not; they were far too much preoccupied. . . He heard Harry speaking volubly, saying, in a tone of irritated apology and explanation—

"My dear girl, I do wish to heaven you wouldn't take it like that. I haven't changed—I never shall. I don't care two straws about Miss Walmer. But really, it is such a splendid chance for me! You ought no more to expect me to give it up than any other good business opportunity that might crop up."

"I should never see you again," she answered, her voice broken by sobs.

"Yes, you would. We should be the same as ever. You know we can't do without each other. You're part of my life."

He spoke casually, but with irritation, as if mentioning a self-evident fact.

"Oh yes, you say that," she answered sadly. "But nothing could alter the fact that you wish to be treacherous, and throw me over—and just for money! It's simply degrading. It's all nonsense to say it will be just the same!"

"Well, of course—for a time—immediately after the marriage—it couldn't be; but it would gradually drift into very much the same."

"It wouldn't, even if it could, because I should never see you again," she repeated.

Harry stood up with his hands in his pockets, his shoulders raised.

Romer could see his face quite plainly, and wondered at its hard, selfish, almost cruel expression.

"Well, if you won't you won't," he said. "How can I waste all my life dangling after a woman who is married to somebody else? I should be only too delighted—if I could afford it. But I can't, and that's the brutal truth. And then, you know, there has been a little talk. That mother-in-law of yours has been gossiping about us. Some day, Romer's bound to get hold of it, and then where shall we be? Don't you see, dear," he went on more gently, "this will stop all that? Wouldn't it be better for me to be married—just in this official sort of way—to remain in England, and be able to see you just the same as ever—very soon—than to go out to the colonies or somewhere, and never see you again at all? There's no doubt I've got to do something. I'm in a frightful hole. Seven thousand a year—a place in the country—and a decent sort of girl, dropped down on me, as it were, from heaven! I hadn't the slightest idea of such luck— and hadn't any pretensions to it. But the girl has taken a liking to me, and her mother wants to get her married. It's ugly—unromantic—but there are the facts. If you cared for me really, I shouldn't think you would want to stand in my way."

"Very well, do it, then," she said, drying her eyes. "If you can speak in this heartless way it shows you are very different from what I believed you. But it will kill me; I shall never get over it."

She was rushing away when Harry caught her hand and stopped her.

"Listen," he said, in an impressive voice. "Go to your room, bathe your eyes, and calm yourself down. Make no more scenes, for heaven's sake, and we'll see what can be done."

"Oh, Harry, really—*is* there any hope? Or are you deceiving me again?"

"I've almost agreed to it, you know," he said. "Still, there's not what one could call an actual engagement yet. At any rate, it might be delayed. I'll see; I'll think—really if I weren't so hard up I wouldn't do it."

"Oh, Harry!" A gleam of joy came into her eyes, and she clasped her hands.

"Then you won't worry me any more about it for the next few days?" he asked.

"I promise;" and smiling sweetly through her tears she left him, going into the house. Her room, on the same floor as Romer's, was at the other end of the corridor, so she did not even pass his door, and had not the slightest idea that he was at home.

He was still at the window, looking out apparently at the garden.

Harry gave an impatient sigh, lit a cigarette and strolled off through the garden.

It had been about three o'clock when Romer had come in and sat down by the window. He was still there in precisely the same position at seven, when his valet brought his hot water.

But Romer could not dress and go down to dinner. He could not see them till he had made up his mind what to do. He always thought slowly, and now he was acutely anxious to make no mistake. He felt that by the slightest wrong move he might lose Valentia altogether. That, at least, was his instinctive dread. He sent Valentia a message that he had to go up to London to see his mother, and would be back the next day. He arranged that she did not get the message till he was driving to the station—just before dinner.

He went up to London and stayed at an hotel, but did not go to his mother's, and thought nearly all night till he had made a resolution. Then he slept till nine o'clock, feeling much happier. He remembered clearly that Harry was coming to town and going to the studio on this day, as he often did. He calculated that he would be likely to arrive by the quick early morning train, and was standing waiting at the door of the studio at twelve o'clock when Harry drove up, looking intensely surprised, with hand outstretched, cordial and delighted.

"My dear fellow, how jolly of you to remember I was coming up! Come in, come in! I've only got this bothering business to attend to, then we'll lunch together, and go back by the four train, shall we? You won't have to stop on here, will you?"

"I don't know," said Romer, as he followed Harry.

"Your mother's not ill, I hope," said Harry, throwing himself into an arm-chair.

"I don't think so," said Romer; "she's at Bournemouth."

"Bournemouth! How like her! But you haven't been down there to see her?"

"No."

"Are you going?"

"Don't think so."

"Then it isn't your mother that brought you up to town, old chap?"

"No."

"Is anything wrong?" asked Harry, after a moment's pause.

It struck him that Romer looked very odd, and as he noted a slightly greyish tinge in Romer's face, he turned pale himself under his becoming sunburn.

"What is the matter?" repeated Harry, who could not be quiet. His weakness lay in the fact that he never, under any circumstances, could entirely "hold his tongue."

Romer put down his stick and hat, which he had been holding, took a chair exactly opposite Harry, stared him in the face, and said in a dry, hard voice, much less slowly than usual—

"There's something I wish you to do."

"You wish me to—"

"Yes. Write to Miss Walmer definitely breaking off your engagement."

"My—engagement?"

"I heard what you said yesterday afternoon. I came back from my walk—there was a nail in my boot. I heard every word from the window in my room."

"You listened?"

"Yes, I listened."

"Romer, my dear fellow, I swear to you that. . ."

"Don't swear anything to me," said Romer quietly. "And don't dare to defend Valentia to me. . . I advise you not."

Harry was silent, utterly bewildered.

"I find that your—friendship, instead of being a pleasure to her, is making her miserable. For some reason she likes to have you about. She doesn't wish you to marry Miss Walmer. Well, you shan't! Do you hear that? You shan't! You're not going to marry that girl and then come dangling about again."

He waited a minute and then said—

"Valentia's got to be happy. You're not going to have everything *you* want. You can surely make a little sacrifice to be her friend!" Then for one moment only Romer nearly lost his control. He said—

"We've been married five years, and I've never said a word or done a thing that she didn't like. And *you* made her cry. You! You made her cry!"

"My dear Romer, I assure you it's all. . ."

Romer interrupted him in a low voice, impatiently.

"Oh, shut up, will you? I want no talk or discussion. I want only one thing. You're to write immediately, definitely putting an end to this engagement. While you write the letter I'll wait, and then I'll post it myself. Will you do it?"

"My dear fellow, of course I'll do anything. But how strange you are! I should have thought—"

"I don't want to know what you would have thought, and I don't care a straw what you think of my attitude. On condition you do what I say, I shall never refer to the subject again, and everything shall be as it has been."

Harry was obviously greatly relieved.

"I will do whatever you wish," he said, looking and feeling ashamed of himself.

Seeing that Romer was evidently in a hurry for the letter, he drew writing materials to him.

Then Romer said—

"One more thing. You are not to tell Valentia anything about this. She's not to know I overheard. I won't have her distressed. Remember that."

"I give you my word of honour," said Harry.

"Very well. And when I've posted the letter we'll wipe out the whole thing. Don't even say you saw me in town."

"Of course I won't."

As Harry bent his head low over the writing-table, Romer, who was sitting motionless, looked at a curious dagger that was hanging on the wall, with a horrible sudden longing to plunge it in Harry's neck. . . Horrified at his own fancy, he looked away from it and thought of Valentia. Valentia would smile and be happy now, and everything would go smoothly again. He would not have to say anything painful to her; she would never be uncomfortable in his presence. In time she would probably grow tired of Harry and could turn to him, Romer, again, with more affection than if anything painful had passed between them. . . His attitude had been extraordinarily unselfish, and yet it had its root in the deep scheming selfishness and subtle calculation of the passion of love. To get Valentia back, as he vaguely hoped, some time, however distant, he had acted most wisely, and he knew it. For he cared for her far too much ever to have conventional thoughts on the subject. It never even occurred to him to try to act as the husband ought to act, or as by the incessant insidious influence of plays and novels most of us have been brought up to think he ought to act. Most people are far more guided than they know in their views of life by the artificial conventions of the theatre and of literature, or by tradition. In fact, most people are other people. Romer was himself. He thought simply for himself, like a child. And so it happened that he acted in a crisis terrible to him, more wisely for his own interest than the most sophisticated of men. . .

"Here is the letter. Will you read it?"

Romer read it and put it back in the envelope. Then he said—

"All right. You're going back to the Green Gate this afternoon?"

"If I may."

"I shall be back tomorrow," said Romer, in his ordinary voice.

Harry accompanied him to the door and held out his hand.

Romer hesitated a moment. Then he said—

"Good-bye," with a nod, and went away, taking no notice of it.

"By Jove!" said Harry, to himself.

XXXV

THE LIMIT

Romer went back to his hotel that evening feeling happier than he had ever expected to be again. He felt sure now that everything would be perfectly right. He refused to allow himself to dwell for a moment on possibilities, and on what had been, or on what might have been. But he was like a man who had been slightly stunned by a blow on the head and was beginning to feel the pain the next day. Yet the pain was not very acute; he did not quite realise it, but, unconsciously, it made him feverish. And he was still a little stupefied. It did not occur to him to go to the Club, or to look up any friends, and he remained in the little hotel in Jermyn Street, filled at this time of the year principally by Americans, and he dined alone there—dined well, and smoked a long cigar. Then he went for a walk. London at the beginning of August was not empty, but stale, crowded, untidy, hot—unlike itself. He tried not to think of the garden of the Green Gate. Suddenly, with a stab, he imagined Harry and Valentia; probably now he was telling her that the engagement was broken off, and she was smiling and happy. Well! it was what he wished. Since what had happened he felt his great love for Valentia was much less vivid than it had been. He cared for her more remotely. She seemed at a great distance. He thought that he felt more to her as if she were a dear sister and living far away. Yes, that was it; he loved her now like a sister.

Surprised at his own calm, and much pleased with his behaviour in the matter, he retired to bed. The instant he had closed his eyes he seemed to see, with the clearness of an hallucination, Harry's head bending low over the writing-table, and, hanging above him on the wall of the studio, the curious dagger; a Japanese weapon that was one of Harry's treasures. And Romer felt again precisely the same horrible longing that he had felt that morning at the studio—the sudden longing to plunge it into Harry's neck. Horrified at the fancy and at himself, he turned up the light and tried to read. He could not fix his attention on a word of the article "Silk and Stuff" in the *Pall Mall* . . .

Of course he was not angry with Valentia; how could she help it? She must be made happy. But she seemed dim, distant, remote. It was an effort to recall her face. . . Harry—Harry did not seem very real to him either. It was all unreal. But he, Romer, had done the right thing. Harry would never make her cry again.

Everything would go on as before. And *he* had never said a word that it would be painful for them both to remember. There was nothing uncomfortable between them. He felt she would grow tired of Harry of her own accord, and would then return to him, Romer, with no disagreeable recollection of scenes, nor of their having said horrible things to one another. Yes, he had been quite right. Yet she did not seem to him so near as she used to be. He was not angry with her. . . No, of course not. He was not jealous. Perhaps she seemed more remote, more distant, because he felt a certain coldness, and—yes—the coldness was there because he was a little hurt perhaps. . . And then he tried to go to sleep again. But instantly his insane vision came back, and he got up and walked round the room and tried to banish it. . . At last he really went to sleep, and awoke trembling with horror. He had had a horrible dream. He dreamt that Harry was writing a letter, and that he had taken the dagger from the wall of the studio and killed him. This was simply horrible.

Then he began to realise the reason. It was subconscious jealousy. Then he saw that he had set himself a task too big for him, and that he could not endure to see Harry with Valentia now. It would be impossible to bear it. He would have to tell him to go. He had mistaken his own feelings. What he had heard on the verandah, what he had imagined, could never be obliterated. Indeed, he saw clearly that if he tried to endure it he would break down. The effort would lead to madness.—It was impossible. . . He had sent Harry back to her! He had actually sent him; it was unbearable.

He would go back the next day, take Harry aside, and tell him that he had found he couldn't bear it, and that on some pretext he must go away. He would tell him that he had reached the limit of his endurance and could bear no more. He would never speak of it to Valentia. Valentia would be sad—but that could not be helped. He knew, now, that he could not endure the sight of Harry again.

Having made this resolution, he became much calmer. But the dream recurred each time he went to sleep until, in dread of it, he resolved to sleep no more. His nerves felt shattered.

And then, he began to count the minutes till he could be back at the Green Gate. To see Valentia again and to banish Harry for ever! And all the obvious, human feelings that he thought he was free from had come back. He broke down; bitter tears of self-pity, of sentiment, and of heartbroken humiliation fell from his eyes. He remembered their engagement and their honeymoon, and then the eternal and everlasting amusing cousin; Harry, and his sickening good looks and ceaseless chatter. No more of it, by heaven! It would be something worth having lived for to have no more of the brilliant Harry. He saw now that he had always been subconsciously jealous of him—that he had always loathed and hated him. And rightly, by instinct; for not only had he done the most unpardonable injury one friend can do to another, without a scruple and without a hesitation, but he had shown the same baseness to her. He made her unhappy. He made her cry. He wanted to marry for money and come back again, treacherous to every one—hard, heartless, selfish, vulgar in mind and in attitude to life. Romer hated him.

Well! Romer would tell him that very day that he had changed his mind and that he was to go anywhere—anyhow—only to go. Neither he nor Valentia should ever see him again.

Valentia seemed a long way off. She seemed remote and distant. That was because he was still hurt and angry. When Harry had once gone, perhaps she would seem near again.

XXXVI

RECONCILIATION

Romer had made one mistake in his calculations. He had forgotten that Harry was a talker. He fully believed that the young man would go back and get all possible credit from Valentia for breaking off the engagement, and would adhere to the very letter of their strange agreement. This, indeed, Harry fully intended to do. When he first went back he told her, to her immense joy and satisfaction, merely that he had broken it off. But when some people who had come to dinner had gone away and she and Harry could be alone, the habit of confidential gossip, the habit, especially, of impressing and surprising her, and, above all, the inability to keep to himself anything so amazing, was too strong for him.

Picturesquely, vividly, and quite amusingly Harry told her every word of the story; first exacting a solemn promise not to repeat it.

"Isn't he *impayable*? Isn't he a marvel? No, Valentia, don't look so grave, or I shall think you've lost your sense of humour."

"But do you believe he really thinks—"

"He doesn't think," said Harry, stopping her. "He won't think. You're faultless in his eyes. He would never allow himself to imagine you anything else. Valentia, this is a wonderful situation—you don't appreciate it! It's unheard of! He particularly wished that everything should go on as before."

He took her hand. She immediately took it away and drew back coldly.

"A wonderful situation! Do you think Van Buren will enjoy it?" she asked satirically.

"Van Buren! What on earth do you mean, Val? Do you suppose for a minute that I'd talk about it?"

"I know you will. You couldn't resist it. It's *impayable* you say. . . Oh, but it was mean of you to tell me!"

"Mean!" cried Harry indignantly. "Why, it was very generous! I might easily have pleased you very much more by saying I broke it off quite of my own accord."

"That wasn't why you told me. You wanted me to laugh at Romer and think him ridiculous."

"I don't at all. I was in the ridiculous position. Be a woman of the world, Val. Don't talk bosh! We shall soon forget it happened."

"I shall never forget," she answered. "And things *can't* go on as they were, because I think he's behaved magnificently, because I think he's heroic. And if I didn't appreciate the way he spared me I should be. . . Why, don't you realise what it must have been for him, Harry, to hear every word we said? And yet he didn't try to make me suffer for it!"

"He complained that *I* made you cry!" said Harry with a ghost of a smile.

"Look here, Harry, it's no good. I see I was right about Romer from the first. I married him because I thought there was something remarkable—something finer than other people about him. And I was right."

"If you talk like that, I shall know you're in love with him," said Harry tauntingly and angrily. "*I* was a fool to tell you. You're just upset, my dear," he added, "at the idea of his knowing of the whole thing. By tomorrow, when he comes back, everything will have calmed down."

"I want to be left alone," said Valentia.

Harry was annoyed, for he himself was not just now in the mood for reverie, and even in the smallest things he disliked giving up his own wishes.

"Oh, very well," he said ungraciously; "perhaps it's a pity I wrote the letter."

"Perhaps it is," she answered as she went away and shut the door.

Harry sat up late, swearing at his own indiscretion and the unaccountability of women. But he was not prepared for what followed.

The next morning, as he was dressing, a note was given to him. It said—

Dear Harry,

"After what you told me yesterday, I feel I never wish to see you again. This is not anger; but it's incurable. I can't account for it, but it is there. How you could have been so stupid as to think I could remain with both you and Romer in the house with this knowledge between us, I simply can't understand. How could I help contrasting his generosity with your self-interested selfishness? I am not angry any more about Miss Walmer. I'm quite indifferent. If you married her tomorrow it would give me no pain. The only kind thing you can do for me now, and the one thing I implore, is to go away on any pretext you like and without seeing me again. To put it perfectly plainly, Harry, I have changed entirely since last night. I see everything differently. Everything *is* different. Forgive me, but I don't wish to see you any more.

VALENTIA

"P.S.—I will send your photographs and other things to the studio. I should like you to burn mine, but do not send them back. I don't want to look at anything that reminds me of you. Do not be angry—I can't help it. I am so unhappy.

V

"If you don't go I know I shall be seriously ill."

After reading this letter Harry was probably about a thousand times more in love with Valentia than he had ever been in his life. Indeed, he felt that he had never cared for her before. He pretended even to himself to laugh at it, and walked up and down his room, saying to himself: "What a couple! What a woman! What a man! They're unique. No, they're too wonderful!"

But he didn't succeed in deceiving himself. He *knew* that letter was final. He did not give it up at once. He wrote her three letters. The first, one of indignant reproach: "*You never really cared for me,*" and so forth, which she did not answer; the second, witty and trivial, with allusions to mountains and molehills and tragedy queens; the third, desperately imploring her to see him once before he went away. To the third one she sent a reply, simply saying—

"Please, please go as soon as possible."

After all his emotion and passionate correspondence it was by this time only about half-past ten. Harry packed, dressed, and went off to the station, mad with rage. He left no word for Romer at all. He felt he had better leave all that to the wife. He had lost her absolutely and for ever—and Miss Walmer too.

In prompt response to his wire Van Buren met him at the station.

And what a wonderful consolation it was to tell him all about it!

Certainly no man ever had a better audience; no one more impressed, shocked, delighted, horrified, amused, grieved, pleased and sympathetic ever listened to a confidence. For Van Buren it was as good as a *cause célèbre*, a musical comedy, a *feuilleton* in the *Daily Mail* and a series of snapshots from the homes of the upper classes—all in one. Never in his life had he heard anything so intensely English. The story gave him the acute, objective, artistic joy that one takes in the best literature, an intellectual pleasure that is usually more or less mingled with the merely spiteful satisfaction that we are accused of taking in the misfortunes of our best friends. And how well Harry told it!

His style was perfect. It was brilliancy, charm, humour, and pathos; he laughed at himself, and yet made himself an object of real sympathy, without losing either his dignity or his dash.

He knew that his confidence aroused enormous interest, and to him that was a great gratification. And so Harry drowned his sorrows in talk, as other men drown theirs in wine, or in sport, or in taking some violent step. He intoxicated and soothed himself with conversation.

But Harry was not an unpractical man—not one of those for whom words take place of actions—and he could face facts. Valentia was irrevocably lost to him. To attempt to regain Miss Walmer, although it might perhaps not be impossible, would make him ridiculous. The letter he had written at Romer's dictation had been too definite. He would give himself away hopelessly as a fortune-hunter if he tried to go back on that. Besides, he was absolutely sick of it all, and if he was more in love with Valentia than he had ever supposed himself to be because she no longer wanted him, he disliked the thought of Miss Walmer far more than he ever had before, because he was convinced she would forgive him and be devoted to him even now.

Van Buren had taken the knock, as he expressed it, using with relish the English slang phrase, with regard to Daphne, and he had made up his mind to return to New York. Under the circumstances he now had little difficulty in persuading Harry to come out with him right away. He undertook to provide for his friend's future, and that he should make a fortune in the Bank, and perhaps when this was agreed upon Van Buren had never been so happy. He was far more genuinely a man's man than was Harry. He regarded women from the point of view of the well-bred American—with deference, a sort of distant tenderness, a most chivalrous and gentle respect. He looked upon them as ornamental and as delightful adjuncts to life, like flowers in a ball-room, but not seriously as part of it. Nor, either, as mere toys. He placed women far more highly than Harry did; he thought everything should be done for them, given to them, that they had a right to any position they were able to hold, that they should be treated with reverence, consideration, liberality. . . and even justice; but—he could do without them. Harry couldn't. And so they would always continue to fall in love with Harry, and to find Van Buren a little dull.

When Romer arrived at the Green Gate that afternoon he found Valentia sitting alone in the drawing-room. Her hands were clasped, she had a serious, anxious, thoughtful expression that he had never seen before. He was surprised at the painful start it gave him to see her again, but he came in defying this sensation.

"Hallo!" he said, in what he meant to be a perfectly easy manner.

He glanced round the room.

"Where's Harry?"

"Harry's gone," said Valentia, in a low voice.

"Oh, has he?"

Romer walked to the window. He looked at her dress, a white dress that he liked, but did not meet her eyes. Then he said—

"Oh, he's gone. When is he coming back?"

"Never," she said.

Romer didn't answer, nor ask why.

After a minute he said—

"Where's Daphne?"

"Gone to stay with Mrs. Foster for a week."

"Oh! Who's coming down today?"

"Nobody. I thought perhaps you wouldn't mind—being alone, I mean." She spoke without her usual fluency.

He stood staring out of the window into the quiet, damp garden. Then he turned slowly round and looked at her. He looked at her little feet in their little white laced shoes; at the slim, narrow line of the white dress; at the hands clasped in her lap. . .

And he felt a sudden pang of cruel, realistic jealousy. But he looked at her eyes and saw tears in them, and, pitying her, he crushed it down for ever.

The marvellous instinct with which women are usually credited seems too often to desert them on the only occasions when it would be of any real use. One would say it was there for trivialities only, since in a crisis they are usually dense, fatally doing the wrong thing. It is hardly too much to say that most domestic tragedies are caused by the feminine intuition of men and the want of it in women. Fortunately, Valentia's feeling of remorseful tenderness towards Romer enabled her to read him now. Of course she would have loved to cry, to explain at great length, to beg him to forgive her and have a reconciliation. But something told her that he could not have borne it; that the subject must never be touched; that she must spare him any reference to it— any scene.

So she said nothing.

AND, DURING THE CURIOUS SILENCE, he gradually and slowly took in the soothing facts. He regained his sense of proportion, of perspective. He saw she was disillusioned about Harry; he felt that the infatuation was over; and, what was more, he realised, to his unutterable relief, that she was not going to talk about it. How he dreaded that terrible explicitness of women, their passion for tidying up, their love of labels! He would not even have to hear it called a sealed subject, and he would not have to say anything at all.

HE LOOKED OUT OF THE window again, began to whistle in a slightly embarrassed way, and then said casually—

"Let's come out, Val. The lawn wants mowing."

THE END